MY MOTHER'S SILVER FOX

THE GERMAN LIST

ALOIS HOTSCHNIG

My Mother's Silver Fox

TRANSLATED BY
TESS LEWIS

LONDON NEW YORK CALCUTTA

Seagull Books, 2025

First published in German as *Der Silberfuchs meiner Mutter*
by Alois Hotschnig, 1994

© 2021, 2023 Verlag Kiepenheuer & Witsch GmbH & Co. KG,
Cologne, Germany

First published in English translation by Seagull Books, 2025
English translation © Tess Lewis, 2025

ISBN 978 1 8030 9 596 7

British Library Cataloguing-in-Publication Data
A catalogue record for this book is available from the British Library.

Typeset by Seagull Books, Calcutta, India

For Mercedes

Only at sixty, not until I was sixty, did I meet my *real* father, this Anton Halbsleben in Hohenems, through a theatre usher who was also from Hohenems.

My father claimed I wasn't *his,* but was the child *of a Russian who drowned*. I couldn't talk about him with my mother; whenever I asked about my father, she had another seizure, so I stopped asking. Once in a while, she'd mention him, but only rarely, very rarely. At some point he married another woman, so I have three half-siblings who are younger than I am. Much younger.

In any case, I met him through that usher, Rudolf Radtke's his name, Radtke, who said to me, I know your half-siblings, I'll call them. Which he did and I got a call from the oldest, from Ingrid, who told me I should come see them in Hohenems sometime, that her father would like to meet me.

I drove there. *You can call me father*, he said. I guess he'd forgotten the thing about the Russian and I didn't bring it up. After that, I'd call him once in a while, send a package now and again because I knew he liked chocolate, like I do, and he wasn't supposed to eat it *either*. *Diabetes*. I inherited the disease from him. The neurasthenia, too.

The *epilepsy* I did *not* inherit. My mother got it from some *shock*. Something happened in Berlin and her fits started very soon after that. Via Berlin she went to Hohenems. She *had* to leave Norway or she'd have been shot, according to my father, he wanted *to keep her from being shot*. The reason is that she got involved with a Nazi, with *him*, in fact. He accompanied her part of the way, to Oslo, I think, then she had to continue on alone.

She tried to see him again, at that point I was already around fifteen. They were supposed to meet in Dornbirn in the *Rote Haus* restaurant, it's still there, the *Rote Haus*. She went, but *he* never showed up.

In ancient times, epilepsy was considered the *sacred disease*. Then in the Middle Ages, it was seen as *sorcery*, that is, epileptics were believed to have relationships with the devil because they survived so much. And my mother certainly survived quite a bit. In Norway she was the *Nazi whore*. I went up there with her once. *Get lost, you and that Nazi whore*, I was told. She had a big family, twelve siblings. The grandfather, *my* grandfather, *her* father, was mayor of the town. A few of her relatives had fled to Russia. In any case, they didn't want to see my mother there. And in Lustenau she was the *Norwegian whore* because the women there were convinced she was going to steal their husbands.

It started in Kirkenes, in early '42, and at the end of that year I was born in Hohenems. She was a nurse, and he was wounded. That's how it happened with the two of them.

Then she got pregnant and had to get away quickly. There were a lot of *partisans* among the Norwegians and if they'd noticed . . . It was dangerous for my mother.

My half-sister told me that he'd her brought down from Norway *out of pity*. He accompanied her part of the way, from Kirkenes to Oslo. Kirkenes is the northernmost town. He certainly accompanied her to

Oslo, she told me so herself, *in Oslo, he was there with me.* After that, she went on alone.

It was *Lebensborn* that brought her south to Hohenems. I found this *document* here by chance, it charts the whole journey. It was decided that *Fräulein Hörvold*—her name was *Hörvold, Gerd Hörvold*—that she should be assisted on her journey from Oslo to Hohenems. Her fiancé would accompany her.

Oslo, Copenhagen, Berlin, Munich, Hohenems. The stations, *the train departures and arrivals.* But it all went off the rails, something happened in Berlin. She was *buried alive*, as she put it. She was delayed there a few days because of an injury. But then she continued on to Hohenems. She gave birth to me there and her illness set in but good. She landed, I believe, in a psychiatric clinic or some other place and I was in a home, for about two years. I never found out exactly what the situation was.

The woman who ran the home was from Lustenau I think, and she brought me to a farmer who lived nearby. How I ended up with them—I assume it was his sister who ran the home and she probably thought, we can bring Heinz to Lustenau, too. This sister didn't live at the farm but there was a housekeeper there. No one else. Just the two of them. And then there I was.

Basically, I only understood how things were once I was at this farmer's. He was already an old man, and he had a large map hanging on the wall with *Kirkenes* on it somewhere. He would take my small finger and said, *look Heinz, there's Kirkenes,* and he burned me with his cigar. That's my first memory. We played that in the theatre, too—*where's your mother from, where*—takes my finger and guides it over the map—*from there, she's from there.* No one knows about it now, but it happened, and my mother, she wasn't there.

I lived with this farmer until 1946. *Only then* did my mother come back into my life.

How did you find me?

Through the Red Cross.

In the meantime, she'd also been in southern Germany. I think she was in a relationship there but didn't want to talk about that anymore either. From '46 on we were together. We lived in Lustenau, in the *Post* hotel. At some point she met this Fritz, she met Reinhard Fritz, my stepfather. But until then we were alone, she was alone with me, and that period of time, when we moved from one hole to another, that was the best time. The *Post* was our first stop, right under the sky, in a garret, we had a room at the top of the house. A steep spiral staircase led up to our room. One day she came *flying down* that staircase towards me and we moved out.

Then we were at the *Gasthaus Lamm*, right next door. I remember the place next to the *Lamm* because my mother was more *balanced* there than she ever was later. We lived very much on our own there. There was no one else. We probably got those lodgings through the community, through the local authority. They realized what the situation was with my mother and me. And they knew how ill she was. But once we moved in with Fritz, for them, the case was settled. After all, we weren't the only two who were homeless, there were others, I know. There was also a French woman with her son and a Russian woman with her son quartered there and then they were turned out.

After that we landed with the Hörmoser family. An elderly couple, an elderly Jewish couple. They'd been able to hide during the war. Few had the chance to hide. These two managed it. A small house and small people as I remember it now. Whether or not *that's* how it actually was, well, I was small too.

They'd been able to hide. I learnt this from my friend Walter Fenz. He'd volunteered to enlist with the navy at seventeen. And then he was stationed on a submarine. So he went underwater and went crazy. He had a lot of things he could tell me. He told me about the Hörmoser family too. The reason was he felt guilty, his entire life, until the end. He was the only person I knew who felt guilty as a Nazi. One of the few. I latched onto him. And *he* said that they were Jews and that they later committed suicide, they set fire to their house while still inside. I'd heard they'd committed suicide from my mother too. It's likely—the pressure continued even *after* '45—and things haven't changed.

My mother was very attached to both of them. Although it was difficult since she only spoke Norwegian. She had, rather, an *intuitive* understanding. She couldn't speak with *me* either. When she got to know me, I spoke the Lustenau dialect. She couldn't understand *me* and I couldn't understand *her*. In those critical years, we didn't understand each other, which no one in Lustenau knew. When I spoke with them later, *you're from Norway*, that's all they knew. *You're from Norway*. Yes.

At the Hörmoser's, in their house, there was one more person, a mason who knew my future stepfather. He had a wife who was mentally ill. She was very fond of *me*, otherwise she didn't like anyone. I always got along with the *mentally ill*, and did later as a nurse, too. His wife's name was Anna. She would always walk around at night with a flashlight or a candle, when she was *out and about* at night, you couldn't stop her.

We lived with the Hörmoser family along with Oswald Bliem. It was through Oswald Bliem that my mother met Fritz. I was around eight years old when we ended up with him. We were finally done moving and *only then* was my mother acknowledged in Lustenau. Fritz was well known. Everyone on *Holzmühlestraße*, they were all related to him, the street was filled with his siblings. They were twelve brothers and sisters. Each one had been given a plot to build on and they all built. That's why the area was known as the *Desser colony*. Apparently, their grandfather always said *des* for the article *das*. That's where *Desser* came from.

There's no one left from that time. The people who lived there were the ones who built those houses after the war. They'd be about as old as my stepfather would have been now, 120 or even older. He was one of the younger ones, I think. These were people who survived the war, many of them were serious alcoholics and were missing a hand or a foot or an eye. Or it was their soul that was mutilated. Not all of them, but many. Before long, they died too. In the fifties, they all died off pretty quickly.

My stepfather, he didn't fight in the war. He was born in '01, already too old for the war and too broken down. He was *undone* by the *First World War* and already ill when I moved in with him. Lung disease. When I met him there was only half of him left.

Why did my mother latch onto this man? Because she wanted to finally have a home for me. He was sick but he was very handsome. My mother was infatuated with Charlton Heston and my stepfather was his spitting image. I remember, when he died, after he was dead, I wanted to take my mind off everything, so I'd go to the cinema no matter what was playing. They showed *The Big Country* with Gregory Peck and Charlton Heston. I saw him on the screen, larger than life, and thought my father had risen from the dead.

As for my mother's *looks*, I only became aware of them after I met Fritz. That was when I noticed she was a beautiful woman. And that's precisely what he was interested in, *the pretty woman*. He didn't care about the epileptic fits. They only started to *bother* him once he couldn't get rid of her, after she got pregnant by him and the fun was over. My brother in '49, my sister in '53. The fun was over.

I'm not leaving you a single pebble, he always said. You won't get one pebble. I first met Fritz in 1949. But I only really noticed him in 1950, when we moved into his shack. And by 1959, he was dead. Still, years enough for him to show me how you kill animals around the clock.

After my mother came and got me from the farmer, we were constantly moving until Fritz. I don't think *she* was even the one who came for me, at least she didn't come alone. There was a woman who helped her, who made sure I was able to get away from those people, and she accompanied my mother a considerable stretch of the way in all the *moves from house to house* that followed.

In the building *next door* to the *Gasthaus Lamm*—it was big and it seemed so empty to me and maybe it was empty—the woman who accompanied my mother, I can see her standing in this empty house, standing next to my mother, talking to her. She was the only one who called her *Gerd*. In Lustenau, they always called her *Gerda*, but her name was *Gerd*. This woman was the only one. Because of this woman I got away from the people on that farm, and it was through *her* that my ill mother appeared. And then—I'm just assuming my mother was in Germany for a while, in Lindau—I'm pretty sure she said *that's where* my godparents were from. They weren't from Hohenems or from Lustenau, they were from Lindau, and I think that's where my mother had been. And maybe it was *them*, my godparents, who brought her to Hohenems and then to Lustenau. I'm imagining it, I *have* to imagine it, or this wouldn't be a novel.

The past is so long ago. A lot is certain and clear—there are documents. But I was just a few years old at the time, so it's difficult: I only know what I experienced *physically*. *That* I do know. But the paths, the detours we followed, even the ones I was there for, those I *have* to imagine. And it's possible that it's *not* my imagination but how it really was: that my godparents brought her to Hohenems, brought my mother because maybe she thought I was still there, in that home or in the town where she left me. And that this woman then happened to appear and told my godparents, *you can go back home now,* and she probably thanked them, *how nice that you brought Gerd here, now I'll look after her.* Maybe that's how it was. But this woman, who I really am picturing right here, in front of me, who then went to Lustenau with my mother, she *must* have known that I was living with that farmer, and she was able to get me away from there by telling him, *the boy's mother is back and I want her child returned to her.* Maybe she even had a position with the authorities, a social worker.

My memory is that she was *there*. She was about as tall as my mother, that I do remember. But beyond that I have to believe my imagination. And it tells me that my mother was in Germany for a while, in Lindau, and that she was in a relationship there. And when it was over, she started looking for me. There are some mothers—it's nothing new—mothers who *give up* their children and don't look for them and don't *want* to hear anything about them. But *my* mother apparently did want to know *if her child, this Heinz, was still around*. So she tried to find out. She didn't want to abandon her child, that much is certain, even if she did say, *Heinz, I don't know if you really are my child or not*. She always claimed that I might have been switched on some changing table in Hohenems. *We're such strangers to each other*, she always said. But there's a reason for that, too, in my opinion. I was four years old when I first met her, that's rather late. I'd been through quite a bit in those four years. *You're not mine. They switched you*, she'd say. That was certainly possible, in the home. Some people deny that it was that kind of a home, a *Lebensborn* home, and some say it *was* that kind of a home. I don't know. There were other children there. Maybe there was *another* Heinz, no one knows anymore. It could be that the woman who ran the home took *the wrong Heinz* to the farmer in Lustenau. Many children were switched back then. Did she get *the* Heinz that she'd brought into the world? Am I him? Am I not? Right after the delivery everything was blank for her, she went straight to the clinic.

At some point later, it was a question of the photograph I found in her suitcase years later along with the *travel itinerary*, the photograph of her and me. Taken when I was a few months old. Whether or not it was *me*—she may well be holding another child on her lap . . . The way she's holding me, I'm two or three months old, not older. She's holding my arm, the child's arm, somehow she's raising his arm, that's how I picture it, I can't remember if it's the left or the right, maybe it's not *Heil Hitler*, maybe, in fact, it's *Heil Stalin*. Maybe she's just propping me up. And this child, in her arms—in any case, she was as *unsure*, this I noticed, she was as *unsure* as *I* am, as I still am today, she was just as *unsure*, too, *is* he my Heinz or is he *not*? She could never say for certain. She only knew the name *Heinz*. But whether he's *the* Heinz she brought into this world, of that she hadn't been sure for a *long* time.

What's clear is that she looked for me, she went searching for me or someone similar and she found *me*. And I wanted to go with her, I wanted to be hers. I liked her sense of humour, her whims, our moving from one place to another, I liked all of it. I also wanted to be sure, *are you the one—or aren't you?*

She was a nurse, they said. They also said that up north in Norway she was a cook. She couldn't cook at all. More than once she put some dish in front of me that was covered in *Ata*. She'd sprinkled the cleanser *Ata* over the food like sugar. Maybe she wanted to get rid of me. *You're not mine. You're not related to me in any way*, is something she *often* said. She would also tell me, *get lost*, or, when she was in a very bad mood she'd call me *Mr. Vicar*. Yes, *Mr. Vicar*. Or *turkey*, because I have such a long neck. Then, she'd call me *sturkey. Get lost, you sturkey, you.* Or she'd chase me with a knife. Often. But she also wanted me to kill her. She'd kneel before me as in a Shakespeare play, holding the knife to her chest and say, *Go on, stab me.*

Everything I later experienced on stage is something I'd gone through *before*. Just much more realistically. Everyone knows that stage prop knives retract.

Fritz's knives were not retractable. He taught me how to kill, my strange stepfather did. There are people who'd like to *interfere* and *persuade* me otherwise. Some are still alive but there's no talking to them. They're no longer all there. And most of those who were *there* don't *want* to acknowledge it. These are *little things*, but for me it was *terrible* that I had to boil the laundry in the wash house because my mother, who was also in the wash house, was always lying down. And then I hung the laundry up over the entire meadow. I wet the bed, at sixteen I was still wetting the bed. My mother constantly wet the bed because of her epilepsy and my two siblings also wet the bed. I hung laundry up in the field all through the year, and *not once* did anyone say to her, *we'll help you.* They only ever said, *you no speak German, you go back.*

I boiled the laundry in the wash house. That's where the butchering was done, too. Everything was done in the wash house. It's a small building. You went down the stairs and into a front cellar. From there you went into the laundry room and on the right there was *another* room, and that's where he kept the chickens.

The house was built in 1950. When the cement was being mixed, I poured in the water from a jug, everything was done by hand, there were no machines. He built it with the neighbour's help. First they built the neighbour's house, then they built his. At some point we moved in and that's when I noticed it all.

My stepfather was always butchering. He would take the animals from the wall. They were all kept along the wall. The stalls lined the exterior wall. There was one stall with rabbits in it. The chickens were kept in the cellar, like everyone kept them in those days.

He always wanted to see blood and taught me how to behead a chicken. I can still see it now, how the creatures ran around, headless, and when I talk about it here, the older folks, they say, *yes, that's exactly how we did it.* It started, the first chickens, how old was I, eight, nine, and the scene—all around me, old women, old people, the way *I am now*, laughing themselves silly. And then: *let them run.* Then the chickens all run around without heads, fall down, get back up. And now they come to me, at night, and jump at me, headless, they jump at my face, these animals that are almost human. And they're right, I killed them. I often have this dream. The creatures spin around, headless, they spin around and jump at my face and I'm covered with blood from head to toe. I wake up, thinking I'm bleeding all over, but I'm only bleeding inside. Nothing's visible externally. Since growing old, I've had this dream.

He also showed me how to butcher rabbits. Butchering, nothing but butchering, beheading, butchering. And these *killing sprees* sent me into a *frenzy*. I couldn't react to anything at all, I was pure aggression. Around me, people lived dangerously. And I lived dangerously with myself.

We were finished with all the *moving*. So I relocated *internally*, from one hiding place to another. One place was my mother's room when she was out, the room that was hers and his.

I was drawn to her suitcase. A small suitcase, only big enough for a few pieces of clothing, probably what she had with her on her journey back then. She arrived with this suitcase and that was that. I opened it and what I found was this photograph of her and me or *whoever*, and this *Lebensborn itinerary*, which the *SS* drew up for her trip to the hell of Hohenems. I never talked about it with her. She would have shredded it, I knew. It would only have ended in a fit. Whenever I *drilled* her about my *real* father, she immediately fell to the ground. But I also found a small book in the suitcase, a chapbook, actually, in Norwegian, and she was very happy to see it. *Peer Gynt*. The play. I found *Peer Gynt* in her suitcase. One day, I put it on her lap and asked her to read from it, out loud, for me. Which she did. I didn't understand a single word and yet I understood everything.

My mother played Åse, Peer Gynt's mother, for me, she did the scene of his mother's ascension, when she rises up to *heaven*. This is the scene she played for me. Again and again, she would ascend to heaven right before my eyes and I couldn't get enough of it.

Later I learnt that an uncle of hers had run a very good amateur theatre in Kirkenes. My mother was an actress, she *would* have been one and whether I'm *hers* or not, what I *do* owe her is the fact that I am the way I am. She read out loud to me and by doing that, she took me away from that place into a world that hadn't existed before, not for me. In her room, on her bed, with this book in her lap, through her *acting*, she brought me into this world second time. *My second birth*, and *this* time she definitely was the mother and *I* was the right one. It was her, it was me, and that's how the two of us were from then on. Before my eyes, she ascended to heaven and through that ascension I came *to life*, at least I did for the duration of a performance. Our own world came out of her suitcase, out of a book, and out of a story about a mother and her lost son. From that point on, this world was our refuge, and having an entire world as a refuge was certainly not nothing.

At twelve, I gave my first performance. I'd built myself a stage behind the house. My mother gave me some old curtains and my first spectators came, my best friend Herbert, who later took his own life, and Erwin, who also took his own life, who jumped into the *Rappenloch gorge* near Dornbirn, that terrible gorge. A few others were there as well, a handful of people, and in front of them I invented my first *stories*.

The house had only recently been finished, and I used the construction material lying around to build that stage in the courtyard, my first *public hiding place*.

I was twelve years old. I was strong at twelve and for me carrying ten roof tiles or the heaviest bricks, without gloves, was no problem, I was used to it. My stepfather had trained me and the neighbours had trained me too. These neighbours were the characters in my first plays. They *appeared* on my stage and over time this *wore them down*. They changed, I noticed, and I changed, too. I also became someone else through these performances. In my first stage piece, I played an *Übermensch*, someone in whom all powers were united and all I presented were horrors. I even maimed myself. I pounded on my own fingers with a hammer. My first play, the first sentence of my first play: *This is how you pound schnitzel.* I had a *meat mallet*, and I pounded my fingers with it until they were bloody. Then from the audience I heard, *stop it now, you're going to kill yourself.* Shortly after that I split my head open or rather *wanted* to split it open. I didn't quite manage it completely.

I performed *above*, in the courtyard behind the house. And my father, my stepfather butchered *below*, in the wash house cellar. The only thing missing was for me to cut off the chickens' heads on stage. I was bloodthirsty. Beheading chickens had instilled a bloodlust in me. When my stepfather had a rabbit in the wash house, he ripped the skin off it—the animal was still twitching—he tore out its heart and ate it, *in front* of me. He made me watch. He forced me: now *you* cut off the hens' heads, it goes quick, you'll see.

Then I did the same, I also ate a rabbit's heart. It wouldn't have bothered me at all to stab the nearest classmate. I'd been taught—by the neighbours, too—how to dash kittens, little creatures, on the flagstones. Old women, my stepfather's sisters, or younger relatives too, cousins, and their children, who were significantly older than me, for them it was all about killing, nothing else mattered. If someone had said the wrong thing, he'd have had trouble getting away. He'd have had to leave very quickly.

You know, Heinz, way too few Jews were killed. And this, this sentence came out of their mouths as if they were talking about lunch. Not just my stepfather, many of them talked like this. And at some point, when you're twelve, thirteen . . . at fourteen I'd internalized it all so thoroughly, that I believed anyone with a different skin colour didn't belong here. *Finding the sore spot and pounding on it*, we had a lot of practice in that, my friends and I.

At some point, it was my stepfather's turn. One Christmas he came home plastered, went into the bedroom and let loose on my mother. He yanked open the window, the candles were lit on the Christmas tree, we were standing in front of it and had started singing, he took the tree and threw it in a high arc out the window. He claimed she was having an affair. He was always accusing her of this. That was when I was twelve. I pulled him off her and flattened him. He gave me my own back, a few days later when I'd come home from school. I was sitting at the table and had just eaten. He came up behind me and almost strangled me. If my brother hadn't been there, I wouldn't have survived. My brother grabbed at him, he was just a little kid, but he grabbed at him so frantically that my stepfather had to let go of me. After that I was afraid of the man. From then on, I always had a knife when I went to sleep, so I could react if he came for me.

And my mother, she constantly had those seizures that left her weaker and weaker. With each attack, a bit of her was lost, and eventually she was *insane*. She too, suddenly appeared next to me with a knife and started chasing me. She chased my friends with one, too. She would change, from one moment to the next, then she really was scary. She fell off her bicycle, she fell in front of a car, she fell into a stream. She wasn't *allowed* to swim. She didn't care, she went anyway.

After my stepfather's death, after Fritz was dead, whenever she made a new start somewhere as a housecleaner or a laundress or a dishwasher, sooner or later she'd fall down and would be sent home. They'd say, we can't have this woman working here, she's always falling down. Once she fell with an iron in her hand and got serious burns on her arm.

Later, I re-enacted those fits onstage. The director said, *we've got to drop that, the audience won't be able to stand it*. It was a premiere. *Please play it differently.* I played it the way *it really was*. The way it was for her.

She read out loud to me. Her favourite scene. In it, Peer Gynt is with his mother, and she starts *fantasizing*. Then she dies. She dies. Then he's alone. His mother's gone.

    That's how it was. In real life, it wasn't any different, because she also died in real life. The *Lebensborn story* and her seizures shattered her. She performed her own death for me in this way, her own death, again and again.

    And, in fact, she *wanted* to die. She would kneel before me, a knife in her hand and say, stab me. She said it again and again over the years. She didn't want to do it *herself*, there were the two other children, after all, she didn't want to abandon them, and that's why she didn't do it. She kept on *for me* and above all she kept going for the two *little ones*, for my sister and my brother. They understood it all, too. I can still see my sister, maybe two years old; or my brother, five or six, always watching our mother *rampaging* on the floor.

Every time, I thought she was going to die. She's leaving, in her own way she's leaving, that's how I felt and that's how it was. It's too much to handle for a child. And then, at some point, she'd get up as if nothing had happened. She'd get up, they'd all get up and life goes on. *Was I gone, was I gone again*, she'd ask. *It started in Berlin and since then I go on the journey.*

Her face twitches, she grimaces, and then the screaming starts, the heaviest tables are sent flying. It's like an *exorcism*, and it is an *exorcism*. Furniture that weighs a hundred kilos starts flying around. And you can't hold her down, either. She won't let you hold her.

She would die in my arms as Peer Gynt's mother and get up again as *my mother*, each time. But then as *my* mother she'd fall down again and be gone, she'd lay there a long time and get up again, and it was impossible to tell when she was *acting* and when she wasn't. She was *there*, but unreachable.

No one knew where her *journey* took her. But I wanted to *get away from there* too, ideally with her, and so I tried to *go on the journey* the same way she did and practiced *falling down* and *falling over*. I portrayed what went on before my eyes, I *re-enacted* it, actually, as I *re-enacted* everything that scared me in order to get hold of it. No matter how often I witnessed them, her *episodes* shocked me every time. And they attracted me. Everything that frightened me also attracted me and in the way that my mother enacted Åse's ascension to heaven, I tried to accompany her on her *journeys*. I wanted to *understand* and I wanted to feel the *strength* she had in those *moments* when she was *unconscious*.

For a while, I only played *the epileptic*. My mother, my stepfather, the neighbours, my friends, my brother, my sister, the doctors, I myself, we *all* had it, we *all* fell, each in our own way. I saw the *trembling* in each one or tried to see it. I was fascinated by the moment *just before it happens*, the lead-in, when *the* question was asked that could trigger it. *Find the sore spot and pound on it*, my friend Otto always said. I didn't *pound*. I *fell*, but that was *pounding* enough because no one who'd recognized themselves in the play wanted to see it.

When does someone become weak and collapse and how does he get back up, and why, that's what I wanted to know, but above all, where *is* he during that time? And my mother, *where* does she escape to, where is her refuge from my questions about my *father*, about my *real father*, who had made off in *seven-league boots*, leaving her, leaving us behind. I wanted to find that place and the other *places*, the *questions* that could trigger that kind of *escape* in my mother and in the others, too.

Her *attacks* were also a place to hide, I felt. She fell down and was gone. And yet, she would fall down in Lustenau and was still in Lustenau when she came to. Wherever her *escapes* may have taken her, the beginning and end of the *journey* were always the same.

As the mother in *Peer Gynt*, she played dead. In *real* life she did *not* play dead, I believe. In real life she played *being alive* when she returned from her *journeys*. Because, in fact, she remained lying there or wanted to remain lying there. She only got up for us, for her children, maybe for herself, too. And the *waking*, the *return to her senses*, as they called it when her eyes opened again, *now she's returning to her senses*, is what they said. That wasn't *entirely* true, because she didn't return to *herself* when she opened her eyes, she came back to us. She came back to *us*, not to *herself* or to *her senses*. It wasn't the same thing.

Before her eyes, I entered her story and *fell down* in it, and, like her, I came back *to life* after a while and got up again like she did. But I couldn't do it for long because they started saying, *Heinz has it too, Heinz has his mother's illness*. I knew that I *didn't* have it. I was *not* gone. I'd fall down and still be *there*. I'd be *alert*, noticing everything going on around me and inside me. But *she* couldn't tell what was *playacting* and what wasn't either; she didn't understand that I was trying to show solidarity with her through these *episodes*. Or maybe she did realize, but just wanted them to stop, wanted me to stop. *You didn't get it from me*, she said, *because you're not mine*. I didn't feel her *strength* in myself either. It was *different* for her, *hers* were different, she was right. We both fall, but not in the same direction, she said.

And yet, through the acting she gave my soul an outlet. She read aloud to me, that is, she *played* the roles because for her, *reading aloud* and *acting* were always the same. Over time, my listening and watching turned into a kind of *co-acting*. She read aloud for me, in her language, which I couldn't understand, but through her *performance* of the passage, I did understand it, in *my* fashion, by *playing it to rights* in my head, which I had to do because there was no other way to get answers to my questions. And so I reflected on and *rehearsed* and *re-enacted* my *observations* and *conjectures* as long as I had to until they became *answers* that gave me something to go on.

In all this, one thing was certain: I wanted *more* of what I could understand through my mother's *performances*. Soon *I* was the one reading to *her*, telling *her* stories, and *she* listened and watched and understood—or not. Either way, we were both performing for each other. The particular day was *the play* that we experienced together. There were no spectators aside from the two of us. In *this* play there was only my mother and me, no one else, not my siblings, not Fritz, no one else. We were close, at least I felt we were, even if it was a play about foreignness that set us apart and bound us together.

From that point on, I lived two lives, one that was *exposed* and, at the same time, one that was *enacted*, without ever talking about it. *Playacting, performing, pretending, feigning,* as well, perhaps, to get through the day and through the days because what happened around me no longer had power over me, I realized, or at least not in the way it had before. I had become *invulnerable*—at least, I felt that way. My stepfather grabbed right through me when he tried to grab at my soul in the wash house, as if he were reaching through the air that I was for him, and that grew ever thinner for him over the years, suffering as he was from lung disease. No matter how hard he tried, he could no longer get a hold of me. For him, I was no longer there. For him, I no longer existed as the Heinz I was, but only as the *character*, as the role that I *represented* for him and *was performing*.

Without noticing, I had begun to *play* myself, not to *dissemble* but quite the opposite, to show myself and stand up for myself. I would *bring to life* the shell they saw of me with, *whichever* Heinz they expected to deal with in a kind of *performance*, as *theatre*, so that they'd leave me in peace, so they wouldn't disturb me.

And in fact, I was spared more and more, at least that's how it felt for a time. I fooled them and as a result I felt *untouchable, out of reach*, and the others only became harmlessly *accessible* to me through the Heinz I performed for them and whose role I'd taken on.

Aside from the volume of *Peer Gynt* in my mother's suitcase, there were no books in the house. There was the magazine *reading circle*, and we got the copies that were already completely tattered because we had the cheapest membership. The issues were a few weeks old and smelled like money from all the hands they'd passed through. Every week, a folder of magazines came to the house. *Bunte*, *Für Sie* and *Neue Post*. *Stern* was in it, too, which sometimes had *serialized novels*. I read them avidly, I was completely wrapped up in them. The first one was about an innocent man who'd been on *death row* in America for twelve years. This story was featured again and again. Every week there was something to read about this man. If he'd been executed or not . . . at the time he'd already been on *death row* for twelve years, that made a strong impression on me and irritated me anew week after week. I performed this story in my courtyard theatre, too. Every week there was an additional act. Everything that irritated or outraged or even delighted me was performed *for* my friends and *with* my friends or just in my own head. In the process, I tried to find ways and ways out for the people I read about in these magazines. In truth, I was seeking ways and ways out for myself. There were things, possibilities to discover in the lives of these people that were unthinkable in my own. But most importantly, I was no longer looking only at my mother and at Fritz and at my siblings and at the neighbours around me, which had meant I was only looking *at myself and my own story*. Instead, I was now looking *out from myself* and into the lives of others and I could see that we weren't the only ones, my mother and I, instead there were *allies*, like-minded people, and people who were also afflicted, people in greater misery than the two of us. All around the world, there were *wash houses* and *prison cells*, in which one ending or another was expected or hoped for. I played through all of these possible *endings*, each week an additional act, at least one, and with time they became independent of any *source* in a novel, coming instead out of my own life.

My demand for *new material* couldn't be satisfied by the *reading circle* alone. My friend Otto provided a solution. Otto Hafner was the first one to give me *proper* reading material. *Dracula* by Bram Stoker. It even got my mother moving. All of a sudden, she heard screams. It wasn't very late. I lay in my bed and the ceiling opened up, then Dracula himself was at my throat. At that moment, I began to scream. My screams must have sounded especially terrifying. My mother was in the kitchen—it was a small apartment—and came running. She shook me and I gradually came to.

 This story filled me with such terror that I locked myself in my room. Soon locking myself in wasn't enough so I nailed my bedroom door shut and fastened the shutters outside the window with wire out of fear that others in the house could be in danger.

 This didn't escape my mother. For days, she laid siege to my door, pounding on it. And then, who was it who came *then*, right, the neighbour showed up. Artur, Fritz's brother, he broke down the door, *Gerda, you've got to treat Heinz differently, he's truly insane*.

He broke down the door and I lay in bed, in *expectation*, and *shocked* by this story that had so completely consumed me and, above all, that I couldn't get enough of.

Until then my life had passed without any dreams, at least none that I remembered. Now dreams filled my days, fantasies, actually. Suddenly, the ceiling would fall, and Dracula would come and suck from my throat. I almost didn't survive my first book, but I let it happen because *without* this book I certainly would *not* have survived, I sensed that, too. This vampire, this being, this fear, whatever it was, wanted me as a person, wanted the Heinz that I was, in any case that's how I experienced it, fascinated as I was by this story, by the terror in it that attracted me more than almost anything had before. I felt *at home* in this *horror*, I felt I'd *arrived* in *my* way. This world was familiar and strange at the same time. There was a threat and ways to fight it. There was this *being* but also the knowledge that it had to avoid the day, sunlight, and the cross, which made it flinch. And there was the stake you could stab into its heart to make it crumble into ashes.

I always had the book with me. The most important passages were underlined. Eventually the whole book was underlined and filled with my notes. So I *couldn't* give it back to Otto. But he kept giving me books anyway.

Otto grew up in a so-called *sheltered house*. He was a few years older than me and had more experience with phantoms than I did. But he had no idea about the effect the book had on me or what was going on at home. No one knew.

He gave me one book after another. One time it was a novel. *As Far as My Feet Will Carry Me*. Here's something that won't give you *nightmares*, he told me. But every book gave me *waking nightmares,* as did every role in the theatre later. In this way, I dreamt myself into the life of my roles and into life in general.

Dracula wanted me awake. There was no pleasure in it for him when I was asleep. He always came *out of the blue*, I could count on it. The ceiling fell while I lay in in bed. Always the same. The ceiling opens up and he comes at my throat. I lie still and don't do anything. Then I scream and scream. And Mother comes through the door. She knew the dream. And she calmed me down. Then I'd fall asleep. Afterwards, I could sleep. And I had to. Because I had to get up at four. At *thirteen* I earned money at *Fruits and Vegetables*. It lasted until '65. Then it was done. Later I went to Wiesbaden for drama school. But before that I worked in a factory, *after* school. I started at fifteen. The factory was right across the meadow, an embroidery factory, I started at fifteen and said to myself, you won't make it out alive.

Dracula is told through letters, diary entries, telegrams, notes of all kinds. That's what I did at the time, too. I *noted* down what had *occurred* the day before or what we'd been *spared*. I also recorded events that we expected or feared would happen but didn't. This way the events were always present, and I was prepared *in case* I had to react. It was an affirmation that, if things had ever been *good* before, everything could be *different*. Because from one moment to the next, one of my mother's fits or a visit from Dracula might disrupt or destroy everything that might have seemed *secure*, at least for that day.

The *undead* had taken over my stage. We were the *undead*, my mother and me, all of us. *Unsaved*. I'd had that sense for a long time. Now I was certain. We weren't *in life*. I'd always felt I was *possessed* or *haunted* by something. Now I had a name for our situation, our condition and on my stage in the courtyard, I held ceremonies and performed exorcisms. The information I needed for them came from Otto's books.

Dracula was a regular guest. There was no evading him—I made sure of that myself by always locking myself in my room, which also kept the tension high and even raised it, because despite all the fear, every encounter with him was also a pleasure. I watched for any opportunity and was always ready and willing. He was inside me, I felt. He had moved in inside me and the question about my father, about my *real* father moved in with him, too.

There never actually was a *real* father. What there was, was the *question* about him. During one of the *meetings* with Dracula, I had the idea that *he* had bitten his way into my mother's life in Norway back then and I was the result. *That's why* he visited me now, that's what he told me anyway, that's what he told me in my thoughts. He'd looked for me for years and had finally found me. I knew that now, but *only we* knew it, just the two of us and we couldn't tell anyone. No one would understand and they'd only try to separate us.

Once, we were lying down again, he bent over me and was different than he'd been before, something in him was always changing, one face gave way to another and in *one* of these faces, I suddenly thought I recognized my *father*, my *real* father, and with that face he smiled at me for the first time.

Why I believed I recognized him, I couldn't say, but I felt it. I'd never seen him and didn't know anything about him except that he could evaporate into thin air and disappear forever. But this time he'd shown himself to me and I knew he existed. I had him in my blood. After all, he'd drunk my mother's blood. Now my father had come into my life, or at least my question about him had.

For a time, I would always panic when he appeared above me but then I noticed he just wanted the contact. He would lie next to me, talking to himself as if I weren't there, about how he was part of us, of my mother and me, and that he missed us, that he longed for us but that we couldn't be together because he was *from another world*, from another time. From my mother's *Norwegian time*.

He'd fallen in love with her in Norway and she with him, and during her fits, when she went *on the journey*, as she called it, he would pull her back to him, I thought. I listened to him, but I didn't trust him. He could tell me anything at all. *Your mother was one of the Germans' tarts*, he said, adding that he'd been serious about her.

In the novel, Dracula had withdrawn to his homeland Transylvania. I looked for it in my school atlas, the Carpathian range, and in the Carpathian Mountains, his castle.

That my father's Transylvania could actually be found in Hohenems, in the adjacent district, a few bus stops away, is not something he told me, or that it would be some time yet before I'd set out to find him in his castle.

I couldn't very well tell my mother who I was with when she shook me out of a *Transylvanian* embrace, nor could I ask why she always looked at me as if she suspected something and had known everything from the start.

In our way, we fled *towards* each other and at the same time *away* from each other, even *into* each other. When I was acting, I would *slip into* my mother. When I watched her, I was looking at myself. I was inside her. And coming back out, that was a *process* each and every time and it's essentially still going on, even now.

Our joint escape into the *serialized novels*, into others' cells on death row. Into acting. And to the cinema. Into films. She had *season tickets* and took me along on the journey, smuggling me into films that were not rated suitable for minors. Somehow, she always managed to get me in. *The Hunchback of Notre Dame.* She had a good relationship with the owner of the movie theatre, they negotiated at the ticket booth, *fine, go ahead, hurry up, quick, in the middle*, and there I was, enchanted by Anthony Quinn and Gina Lollobrigida and by the whole subject, which was my subject.

I immediately felt sympathetic towards the *bellringer*, who lived up in the tower with his bells, and who'd gone crazy from the ringing.

He couldn't hear a thing anymore because of the bell, *big Mary*, which he rang by swinging on the rope. *She made me deaf,* he said.

I was attracted to Gina Lollobrigida and the *bellringer* was attracted to *Esmeralda*, a beggar, *an Egyptian who grew up with gypsies*, according to the film. She dances for other beggars on the square in front of the cathedral and they cheer. A priest sees her from the church tower and falls in love with her. And the bellringer sees her from his tower and falls in love with her. But she only has eyes for another. The priest tries to kill this man out of jealousy and pins the guilt on *her*. She is tried and the priest—it's his statement that leads to her conviction. She's convicted as a *witch*. My mother was a *witch* too because she made a pact with a *Russian who drowned*.

During the attempt to free her, Esmeralda is killed. Quasimodo looks for her. From his tower he can see her corpse being dragged to the place of execution because she has to be hanged even though she's dead. When he gets there, her body has already been taken down from the gallows and brought to the catacombs below. He finds her body among the other corpses and lies down next to her. Just as Dracula lay down next to me, he lies down next to her. Years later, their skeletons are found. They are *intertwined in a strange way*, and they turn to dust when pried apart.

I thought that if there had to be death, then the story should *continue*, and the next time my mother had an attack, I lay down next to her. Not to turn to dust with her, but to escape, even if just into the next movie and the one after that and so on. We were both addicted to this other world, which was now open to me.

Just as she had at the farmer's house where she came to take me back, my mother re-entered my life in the movie theatre in Lustenau, through the films, during which I could get to know her in a way that was impossible otherwise. The screen on which everything played out was her face, *we* were the screen, and every story that flickered through us became a story about her and about me. We lived many lives, witnessed them in the stories of others and caught up on all we might have missed in the years we were separated.

The bellringer and *Esmeralda*. My mother and me. The roles were assigned. The Norwegian idiot, the reindeer, the Lapp and the *beautiful foreigner* who had the devil in her, the *Norwegian whore*, who not only turned the heads of all the men in the neighbourhood, but also those of my friends, *your mother's beautiful,* they always said when they came over, which in truth, they did to see *her* and to be near her.

She often danced in the courtyard below, like *Esmeralda* on the cathedral square, she danced among the rabbits and chickens and cats in the back courtyard on Holzmühlestraße. She laughed and waved at me up in my room, where I was watching her. What is she thinking right now, I'd wanted to know. Who is she dancing for, who is she thinking of—the beggars of Paris or her friends in Lindau or Kirkenes or Oslo? Or was she thinking of the neighbours in the *Desser colony*? Impossible to say. And it had long been unclear to me *which person I was when I watched her*.

For a time, she played *divas* for me, *Greta Garbo*—she knew all of her films and played scenes from them for me, often for no reason, seemingly disjointed, off the cuff, on the way home from the movie theatre or in the grocery shop, suddenly she was Greta Garbo or Zarah Leander or even *herself* in new *facets* that I'd never seen before. She would grab my friend Hubert or Erwin and dance the Charleston or the tango with him, on the kitchen table, in the courtyard, on the street, no matter what they were doing. Or she would imitate someone if she didn't like them but if she *particularly* liked them, then she'd do it, too. But always so that the one she was imitating didn't notice, wasn't meant to notice, because she did it *in secret*, in a way that was obvious only to my friends and me. We called it her *silent show*.

Those were the days when she had *fair weather* in her head, as she called it, and we were grateful for those days. Because there was always a chance of *lightning*, for her and for anyone who happened to be near her.

When people said a woman was *struck by lightning*, it meant she'd gotten pregnant. *Lightning struck*, was what they'd say. When lightning struck my mother, then the mood changed and a storm set in. Either she fell down like an animal that was *giving up the ghost* or she went *wild* and started fighting against something that none of us could see but which she believed was near each time and which she struggled against as vehemently as if everything depended on it—and so it must have. Then we knew we had to disappear. *Avoid the oak, seek the beech*, because she was the centre of the storm, the source of the lightning. But maybe, in truth, *I* was the cause, and it was no different for my mother than for other women *when lightning strikes*, because *I* was the one, after all, who'd *struck* her in Kirkenes, and every storm and all the bolts of lightning since were a memory of that lightning strike back then.

After Fritz died, when my stepfather was gone, we lived only for the movies at first, *in* the movie theatre, actually, in the movies.

It was over with Fritz and we were also done with the *confessions* whenever we went to see a movie. *Did you break the law of chastity again*, he always asked when we came back after seeing a movie. He didn't like films. He didn't like anything that wasn't about him. Movies for him were rank indecency. The kind of indecency he suspected in everyone who looked at his wife, even if only from a distance, because she'd once been *temptation itself*, as he always said, she'd put a spell on him, that's the kind of woman she was, she couldn't keep herself from doing it. And now that he was ill, others had their *eyes on her*. He was a man like any other, so he knew what *all men* wanted, wanted from her, and probably got, too, according to him. She was under suspicion. And with her, so was I, because I was incarnate proof of the *temptation* that my mother was personified.

Otto had laid the cornerstone of my love for horror. Now this horror wasn't only at home and in books, but also in movies and I was obsessed with horror films. My mother wasn't. I'm horror enough for myself, she said, so from then on, I went to the cinema alone, too.

Frequently, a woman sat next to me when I was there alone. She owned a classic car and drove people around the area in it during the day, and in the evening, she'd sit next to me in the darkness of a horror movie, in the seat my mother had sat in until then. And when the movie was over and the horror vanquished, she'd say, *things like that can happen. Things like that can happen, Heinz*, she'd say every time.

A movie could never have enough horror in it. A mad doctor who does experiments and constantly tries to transplant heads. A man who survives a nuclear bomb test without protection then grows and grows, and the bigger he gets, the more evil-minded and dangerous he becomes. And that woman sat next to me, as terrified and thrilled as I was. She had a taxi—that car from the 30s. And now and then, she drove me home from the cinema in it.

Once my mother had probably had one of her fits in the cinema. The owner came, his name was Oskar, a very nice man, and said, Heinz, I'm worried about your mother. Bad things can happen on the way to the movies, too, after all. She started going to the movies less and less. At some point she got a television, an old TV, and then she was done with the movies.

Day and night that television flickered through her life. Without sound. Whether or not the speaker worked, it was and remained silent. Everything is so loud anyway, the pictures are enough for me, she said. In all the years I visited her later, the television was on around the clock. Without sound. But she wanted pictures of the world, even when she no longer understood anything.

I started school... Let me think... I was born in '42, but late in the year, so I started with those born in '43. Let's see, at what age did we start school then? At seven, so I'd have been eight. My first schoolyear was 1950. I left school seven years later. When I was fifteen. I went straight to the factory, the embroidery factory, to earn money.

And *before that*, in school, the teachers couldn't understand me. No one has any idea what you're saying, they always told me. Between Norwegian and dialect, I constantly confused everything.

Besides, there was no one like me, always taking detours because they all wanted to beat me up. And at some point, *I* started hitting back. After one of them just wouldn't leave me alone. Over time, they stopped hitting me and at some point, they even became afraid of me. I also armed myself—I brought the kitchen knife to school. I stuck it in my schoolbag. And one time, I grabbed one of the girls in my class who always called me *reindeer, reindeer* every time, I held her tight, in the middle of the street, put the knife to her throat—*reindeer one more time*—that girl never called me *reindeer* again. No parents showed up either. They were probably afraid of me too.

Basically, I could have gone and shot them all in a classroom, like those two young men in Germany a few years ago. Or I'm thinking of a story from the 60s, so quite a few years later, I was already on the path of wanting to be *a good person*. But back then, *that* was in the 60s—a young man with long hair is sitting in the Lindau train station. Someone comes up behind him with a bolt pistol, the ones for killing animals, and shoots him. That's what it said in the newspaper *Young Lindauer Shoots Longhair with Bolt Pistol*. I'd have been capable of doing that when I was twelve.

Only my *last* teacher—he was the *first* one who understood me. Anton Schreiber was his name. He knew I was *different*. He sensed it and kept giving me things to read. Because of him I did some catching up. He saw through me, he found me out in my *Heinz act*. He encouraged us to write our *own* stories. Before him, no one had done that, so I wrote a brief *life story* for him. One thing I wrote about in it was the farmer who always burned my hand. I drew a picture on the facing page. I drew an *Übermensch*, just like the one I was *playing* on stage in the courtyard at the time. This teacher also sang, he liked singing with us and wanted to hear my *favourite songs*. And all I had to choose from were the songs I'd learnt up in the mountain pastures. In the summer, my friend Herbert's father took us with him to the high pastures every now and then. He worked up there. His name was Franz. And he's the one I travelled with to *Transylvania* by moped years later. But back then, at that time, I didn't yet know anything about all that.

I hob amol a Ringerl kriegt, von meinem Herzensdirnderl. Und i hob ihr a Röserl geben, grod wie's im Sommer blüht. (My sweetheart once gave me a ring. And I gave her a rose that bloomed in summer.) I sang one of these typical, sentimental alpine folksongs for Anton Schreiber at school. *It's clear the song suits you and it comes from the heart*, he said. There were a few other old songs but this is the one I remembered and later, I sang it on stage too. In *Platonov*. In the play, I was a drunken general who was after his daughter. I always sang such little songs softly to myself when I longed for my daughter. The director told me to just hum the songs, then keep boozing.

But back then, when I was twelve, around twelve and later, there was just the movie theatre, nothing else. There was one place I always liked to go. The *Alter Rhein*. That refuge, too, could have come from a movie. *Tarzan's Savage Fury*. It was the owner of the cinema who gave me the idea. After the last screening I asked him when we could expect another Tarzan. And he replied, ask him yourself, as far as I know he lives not far from here. Why wait for a movie when you've got reality on your doorstep, over on the *Alter Rhein*, he said.

And the woman, the taxi driver, who saw the movie with me and was standing right next to me, said, yes, Heinz, could be. Both of them were right. It's true that Tarzan had left the place—if he ever really was there—but it was his world I'd just entered. A primeval forest, a jungle and not a stage set, not a movie, but real life, for which a script was waiting to be written.

For a long time, I went there every day. Those enormous trees. The undergrowth. It was sheer glorious wilderness, as if made just for me. Lianas hanging down from the trees, which I knew from the films. The monkeys ate them; I smoked them.

I learnt to swim in the water there. I'd go even in the pouring rain, and then I was sure to be alone. Most of all, I liked swimming when there was thunder and lightning. So that it could strike me dead in the water. That's what I always wished for. I got that from her.

The *Alter Rhein* was bliss. And because Tarzan never showed, I gradually tried to take on his roles as best I could. I stepped in for him. For Lex Barker, that is. His was the first role I took over for someone else. As might have been the case many years earlier, though I couldn't have known it at the time, when I stepped in for the *real* Heinz, after my birth, on the changing table in the home, when they presented me to my mother as *her* Heinz. Or again, in the farmer's house, where she came to get me. But this time and now, I knew from the start that I was the *substitute*.

The *Alter Rhein* was my first jungle. I was Tarzan for the first time there.

You look like a nun, my mother always told me. She wasn't wrong. I often played nuns or an elf in *Midsummer Night's Dream*. You've got the face of a nun, she'd say. And I wanted to look like Tarzan, like Johnny Weissmuller or Lex Barker, at least in my jungle days on the *Alter Rhein* I did. When someone had to play a woman's role in the theatre, then I was the one. I didn't need a dress, just my face surrounded by a veil was enough. My mother noticed it first. That's why she always called me *Pastor*. If she wasn't in too bad of a mood, then I was *Reverend*.

Nonetheless, I eventually played Tarzan on stage. The play was called *Tarzan is my Big Brother and Superman is my Best Friend*. The man who wrote it was fond of me. The actor who was supposed to play the lead role and who would have been ideal had to drop out. So the playwright came to me and said, Heinz, go on, take the role, it's just a children's play. Do a few push-ups now and then, and you'll fit.

At the time, I was doing karate because I'd been killing myself with drinking. The doctor told me, get yourself on the national health plan, they cover athletics, otherwise you won't live much longer. And so I ended up at that karate school in Saarbrücken. There I did push-ups until I was Tarzan. *The way Heinz Fritz moves his abs is impressive*. One of my best reviews. The director said, *Mr. Fritz, you're not ideal, but you make a real effort*.

The way things look on the *Alter Rhein*, in Lustenau, it's all completely different now. The movie theatre isn't the way it used to be either. I performed there just three years ago. It was called *Rheinlichtspiele* back then. *CinemaScope*, enormous screen, large theatre. It's been divided into three or four small theatres now. I didn't recognize it when I came back.

Tarzan's Savage Fury. The *Alter Rhein* didn't need a savage protector, definitely not me. There aren't any more lianas there now. Being at the *Alter Rhein* was the best time of my life. Happiness grew down from the trees and I smoked it.

Just a few years earlier, refugees had crossed the border there. New refugees kept coming, trying to cross the border, and were shot as deserters. It was easy to cross the border there, you could wade through the water which was often only ankle-deep. But then the border guards came and killed or stopped them.

From the bank you can look across the river to Switzerland. For a while the SS led Jews across for money. They guided around six hundred people, some of the SS men said after the war. If true, then they saved people.

In the middle of the river, you were already on Swiss ground. On *our* side of the river, you were sent to the camp, to Theresienstadt.

And fifty meters from there, freedom began, or could have begun, since many were sent back. In Switzerland there was Paul Grüninger, who saved many people against orders at the time. *Diepoldsau* was the name of the community. *Diepoldsau.* The border police were stationed in Hohenems. Fifty officers.

I heard of one instance in which a refugee was saved. A German who was in a dispute with his landlord crossed the border there. A man in Hohenems hid the German for fourteen days until he could cross. The man had conspired with a border officer and had given him, the German, a scythe. They went to the *Alter Rhein* and did field work there. Then the man said, *and now, run, fast. Jump.* And when the German was on the other side of the river, the man called the border officer who was on duty that day and nearby so that he, too, could pretend he was helping with the mowing. In the meantime, the German was gone. There were some people who helped but no one ever knew about them. Or that someone might really risk his life for Jews—there were some people like that. And there were others, especially the SS, who wanted money and were happy, up to a certain point in time, when Jews crossed the border because they could earn something helping them. Later, they just exterminated them.

There are no more lianas there now. I always found them calming. Sometimes I bought a pack of *Donau* cigarettes. My mother smoked *Donaus.* But I never had the money and the lianas, I thought, were wonderful.

I still remember who gave me the idea. There was a Capuchin friar, living outside at the *Alter Rhein*, who sold chestnuts. Summer and winter, he was always there. He often gave me a cone of chestnuts. He stood there on the path, in his robe, all alone. In his own way, he'd *left the order.* And he said, for some reason he said to me, I couldn't manage there any more and now I'm living my life, here, on the *Alter Rhein.* He had a small tent that he lived in. And then, later, he also had a small canopy, under which you could sit and eat the chestnuts.

This Capuchin gave me the idea. He'd smoked them. I asked him, what's that? Well, they're lianas. *Niala*. He didn't speak dialect, as I recall. Somehow everything he said was high German to me. I don't think he was from another country.

The robe—this I remember—it protects me like a tent, he always said. But once in a while, you've got to leave your tent. There are times when I have to get out.

I saw this friar whenever I was there. I passed him on the way to the jungle. Then he'd offer me a few chestnuts and I'd listen to him. And he to me. Sometimes I paid him. Then he'd say, there's no need. Whether he still had anything to do with the church is not something we ever talked about. But it was clear that he wanted to live his *monk's life*—that he wanted *to continue his monk's life*, in this way. His tent was nearby, behind the first trees, near the water.

There were stories about how Jews waded through the water, crossed the border and were shot and killed. These stories were told discreetly and if you asked for more information or wanted details, there was nothing more to learn. I heard some stories, but only in scraps and mysteries. There was one that must have been particularly brutal, a man from Lustenau shot one of these people *at the Rohr*, that's what the place is called, *at the Rohr*, a canal pipe over and through which many Jews escaped to Switzerland. I tried to find out who the man was who shot the person escaping. But they all stopped talking, *some things you don't need to know, some things you don't need to know*, they all said in dialect and abruptly *shut me down*. But it definitely happened.

There's another person who helped me a lot and to whom I owe *everything*, a chaplain who was completely different from the others. He recognized my *inclination*, how I sang and wanted to become *someone else*. He gave me a small accordion. And my very first evening, at the time we were all in the *Young Catholic Workers*, down below, in the cellar, there was a small stage, and he set up my first performance there. I sang some songs, those old songs, and improvised on the accordion.

I didn't have a music teacher, I taught myself. I sang the songs I'd sung in school, *I hob amol a Ringerl kriegt, von meinem Herzensdirnderl*, the sentimental alpine folk songs I learnt from my friend, from Franz, who'd then come with me to Hohenems. He was an Alpine dairy farmer and he always invited me up to the summer pastures. Sometimes Herbert wasn't there and I was alone with his father. At night after the cows had been milked, there was a very spooky atmosphere. Franz would light a candle and start singing. Those folk songs sound sentimental and usually have sentimental endings. Either the shepherd dies or the shepherdess does. *Someone always dies*. I sang this song in my first performance. Then I sang another song, one that everyone knows, that goes like this: *In Mueders Stübele, do goht der hm, hm, hm, in Mueders Stübele, do goht der Wind. Tralalala hahaha, tralalala hahaha, tralararo.* (In mother's little parlour, you feel the hm, hm, hm, in mother's little parlour you feel the wind. Tralalala . . .) A crazy song, it could have been written by Karl Valentin or Otto Grünmandl. People always sang it in Lustenau when they were drunk. Still, better than always *Raise the Flag High*, I thought. I sang those two songs and told stories. The chaplain arranged it. He's the one who got me started. Unfortunately, he was suffering from lung disease. I learnt this later. He was already emaciated when I got to know him. A very fine human being. Like the friar, the Capuchin on the *Alter Rhein*, who always gave me chestnuts.

The chaplain had taught religion in the school. *But religion includes singing*, he always said, and *playing football is also a kind of prayer*. We did that, too. He accompanied us out into the Rhine River basin and there, divided into two teams, we *prayed* while *playing* against each other. He couldn't play, he was too ill. He would sit, very pale, on a rock that had been placed there as a seat, and we would play. He managed to get the football for us, he probably paid for it himself, a leather football, which was something special in those days.

Again and again, people like him came into my life. Without these people, I probably would have ended up as a murderer. Had there not been such moments, I would have exploded, I think, without men like this chaplain or the Capuchin friar, who was just there, like a tree on the way to the *Alter Rhein*, in whose shade you could rest. I saw him regularly for years and suddenly he was gone. I asked after him but no one could tell me where he'd gone.

He had left the Capuchins. *I'm no longer in the Order*, he'd say, *but they let me keep my robe.* He had lived in that robe and sold chestnuts to survive and to help others survive because maybe these chestnuts were just an excuse to talk to vagrants like me.

Hansel and Gretel. Otto had the right book for the *Alter Rhein*, too. *For your lending library*, he said. One day, the parents take their children into the forest. I wasn't at all surprised to learn that the parents had taken their children into the forest to abandon them there. The malice with which they did it irritated me, the way the father hung a piece of wood from a withered tree so the wind would knock it against the trunk. The children who were some distance away thought the father was still chopping wood long after he and their stepmother had run off.

That was not going to happen to me. As a reminder I tied a piece of driftwood I'd found on the riverbank to a withered tree and knocked it against the trunk for hours at a time so that I wouldn't forget what to expect if I ever had to depend on someone utterly. I can still hear the knocking today if anyone tries to get too close to me. I had no parents close to me. I couldn't bear being close to my friends for long either. I ran away from Herbert and from Erwin. Just as my mother had too, *send them away, send them all away*, she said when anyone wanted to visit her, up until the very end she said this. I was no different. And however much I wanted to be close to her, I had to get away from her, too. The *Alter Rhein* was such an escape. With that piece of driftwood, I beat my own presence into my mind along with the absence of everyone else. Only my friend, the Capuchin, was allowed to hear that I existed and that I was with him in my thoughts and I still am, to this very day.

Switzerland began in the middle of the river, not fifty meters from the bank where I'd made my camp. At the spot where the refugees crossed the border through the water.

And if there were some things I didn't *need* to know, I still wanted to *feel* them. *Crossing the border*—how it feels. Above all, *what exactly is* the border. You can't see it in the river. At first, I crossed it at night, in the dark, and as time went on, I also crossed during the day.

But this border wasn't visible, it was as if non-existent. And you couldn't *feel* it either. I couldn't. The water on the Swiss side was just as cold and just as deep as on our side. Still, for the refugees back then it was the difference between life and death, between freedom on the other side and deportation to a camp or Theresienstadt on our side. But I, at the time, couldn't feel the difference, nor did I understand the difference a border makes.

My mother crossed the visible border. Once a week, she crossed a bridge into Switzerland to do her shopping, at least that's what she said. And just as she always came back with one or two hidden packs of cigarettes, so I smuggled myself a few hundred meters over the water into Switzerland and back, intent only on not getting caught, though actually, in fact, I was really intent on getting caught after all and finally being exposed as the secret *Norwegian* that everyone here believed me to be. After all, something had to happen, something that wouldn't otherwise happen, that's what I wanted to provoke. Maybe also so that I wouldn't have to go back, back to *Fritz territory* and to finally cross the border, any border.

Of one thing I was sure: I was at home in this wilderness. I caught fish myself. The campfire. The lianas. The fairy tales. And all of it always *on my own*. That is, not completely alone because in my head I was *only* with others.

For a long time, my plan was to set up a camp on the Swiss side so I could go to ground there, if ever necessary, or to stay there one day and go on from there, maybe all the way to Norway.

Did my mother cross the water, too? On her itinerary, there are two mentions of ferries. But at the end of her journey, she reached Hohenems via Lindau. She had fled *into the Reich*, not away from it. My mother had fled the Norwegians south to Hohenems, to the place from which all those people who tried to cross the border at the *Alter Rhein* wanted *to escape from*. My mother, with me in her belly, was heading in the opposite direction. That's what was written on that yellowed, wrinkled scrap of paper that I found in her suitcase and that I always had on me during my searches. I guarded that itinerary like a passport, which I didn't even have at the time. No. *My* mother had come *from the other direction*, from the *opposite* direction. She fled *to the Nazis*, not *away from them*.

These thoughts came to me in the forest on the Swiss border and with the map that my teacher Anton Schreiber had given me open on my lap. One day, he gave me another book and in it I found the map, a kind of bookmark. *Those who don't know where they come from should know where they want to go*, he said to me when I tried to give him back the map.

On this map, I traced her journey from Norway south and imagined traveling in the *opposite direction* one day. The towns, the names of the places, the stops *were in my blood*, I'd studied them so often. I'd list them like a counting rhyme. Hohenems, Lindau, Munich, Berlin. Hohenems, Lindau, Munich, Berlin. Something happened in Berlin. From Berlin, I'd go on to Oslo and from there on to Kirkenes. Hohenems, Lindau. Lindau, Munich. Munich, Berlin. Berlin, Warnemünde. Warnemünde, Gedser. Gedser, Copenhagen. Copenhagen, Elsinor. Elsinor, Helsingborg. Helsingborg, Halden. Halden, Oslo. Oslo, Kirkenes. I repeated these names incessantly to myself as I swam across the Rhine to Switzerland and back.

When I came home from my trip and my mother was waiting for me on the front steps, *where did you go this time,* how could I tell her that I'd crossed the border and had been in Berlin, had been with her in Berlin since she was always with me on my journeys, always with me, everywhere. And that I'd gone on to Oslo and farther north and that's where I'd come from. And that I now knew this stretch *inside out* I didn't tell her, just as she never told me anything. But I thought to myself that we have the *same* secret and on top of that we are keeping the same secret from *each other*. My plan was to prepare myself to tell her one day and together we'd take off given that we didn't belong where we were.

Next to the withered tree to which I'd tied the piece of driftwood, there was an anthill that had grown over the years to be as tall as a man. It had been there from the beginning but it kept growing, it didn't stop growing. And it moved, too. The creatures had probably taken over the tree and hollowed it out over the years. There was a constant back and forth between the tree and the anthill, and it was impossible to say if the insects came from the tree or if this steadily growing hill was the nest from which they all came. The bigger the anthill grew, the more it seemed to move, to expand. It shifted, unnoticeably, but still constantly. Because I was there every day, the changes were hard to recognize, but finally, the anthill had moved so close to the trunk that it completely surrounded it. I'd set up camp nearby since I was particularly drawn to this place. The creatures' supposed turmoil always calmed me.

With the map open on my lap, I sat next to the pulsating anthill and studied my future trips into my mother's past. One time, I stabbed the anthill with a stick. After a time, the spot came to life, masses of ants swarmed out of the crater that I'd drilled into the hill, and they spread out over the entire area and over the map which I'd let drop. In ever new waves, they ran over the countries as if in a panic, across Europe and beyond in a teeming confusion, many of them carrying an egg in their mouths, of which I was one. It was no different, wherever they were, wherever the Germans were back then, there were also children they'd conceived, *Lebensborn children* as well, of course, and the mothers, who tried to bring them to safety. I, too, was an ant egg. My mother was a *Lebensborn ant*, who'd left her Norwegian den and set out with me into this confusion. There isn't one single *Lebensborn path*, each woman had to find her own way. My mother wasn't alone in this, that is, she was left on her own like thousands of others.

There were also *a few* soldiers who had wounded or shot themselves because they didn't want to continuously keep killing Russians or Jews, because they didn't want to murder any more French or Yugoslavians and Greeks and didn't want to wipe out the whole world anymore. There were a few of these here, too. And there was a certain Otto Neururer in Götzens near Innsbruck who'd saved people or had tried to, who had stood up for Jews and was killed for it. From here I can almost see Götzens. He'd lived *within eyeshot*, these people could be found and still can be found within my range of vision, and they managed to save just enough people so that not *all* were murdered.

There was Otto Neururer and out on the *Alter Rhein*, on the Swiss side of the border, there was Paul Grüninger. He saved around two thousand people, we know of them because he didn't hand them over to the Swiss authorities or send them back—even though the boat was *full*, overloaded, as they said at the time. At least Grüninger didn't die the way the priest Otto Neururer did, hung upside down in *Buchenwald*. Although Grüninger was destroyed psychologically over decades for rescuing those people. He was not forgiven in his lifetime.

At the *Alter Rhein* I could always gather strength with the Capuchin. I was either at the *Alter Rhein* or at the cinema, at the *Rheinlichtspiele*, where they showed the films that were an important distraction for me. Now it's the *Kinothek*, but a lot of people still go there, and some of them, certainly, for the same kind of *escape* and *return to themselves* or just *to get away from themselves*, at least for a time.

The *homeland* in the films of the era, those so-called *Heimat* movies, was never a homeland for me, one that, given everything that had happened in the prior years, *no longer* existed, was forgotten and that, in fact, these films were intended to make us forget. It was often hard to bear the laughter in these *Heimat* movies. The grin-and-bear-it-laughter of the war years became a post-war-reconstruction-laughter, an economic-miracle-laughter. But the forgetting and the fostering of forgetting remained the same.

I didn't lose my ability to laugh because of this, nor did my mother. Even though she was in a complete despair at the time—the epileptic fits, Fritz and Fritz's illness, her young children and me, especially me—she sometimes lay there drunk, just as I did even when a child, in the cellar, she lay completely sloshed and tried to put an end to it. She lay in the wash house, in the bathtub, in the same washtub Fritz used to collect the blood from the animals. She lay in the tub as if in her own blood, the water *trembled* around her in that underground jungle. I saw her through the half-open door. She lay in the water and waited, hoping she'd have a fit and drown. She tried again and again, just as I'd tried when I was twelve, when Herbert saved me because he happened to come by. He'd wanted to see me and first stopped in the kitchen where my mother probably said, Heinz must be downstairs, which was the case. I wanted to split my head open. I sat in the cellar, in the tub, and gave myself unbelievable wounds. With the hatchet.

Mother sensed that something was wrong and came down the stairs, I can still hear her steps. I had closed the door, a very heavy door.

Mother called and called. Who broke down the door? My best friend, who later hanged himself. Six years ago. We were the same age. My head wasn't *completely* split open, but it looked bad. It looked very bad. They drove me to the doctor in a trailer, in a fruit trailer. He *stitched* me back together.

Acting always healed me. Even if only temporarily. Through acting, I *tricked* people and evaded them by being for them someone I wasn't internally. I learnt to be *different*, to leave myself behind and yet to stay *with myself* and in this way to ultimately become *myself*. Through this *transformation* I could feel a kind of *pleasure* that I gave *others*, and I pursued this pleasure as a *game* and I knew that *I* was the one playing and this turned my compulsion to *disguise* into a delight in *displaying*.

Herbert often joined me in these *displays*. He had a good voice and we were invited to sing in taverns. *Moonlight* by Ted Herold was my biggest hit, it still is. A lot of other pop songs. Evening entertainment. We were a good duo and good at this too. He knew the song *Mamatschi, give me a little horse*—people had tears in their eyes or Vico Toriani's hits, he could sing them in all pitches.

That was always during vacations, when I would still go back home, we would always sing. Until it didn't work anymore. It started very early on, his not wanting to sing, his not being able to, actually. *You don't understand me, Heinz, like the others you don't understand me.* His brother hanged himself, too.

Lustenauers are very gloomy, like all Alemanni. And I'm twice as gloomy, because Norwegians are *even* worse. They can barely walk upright, their spirits are so heavy. They carry entire boulders around with them. I didn't see a single happy Viking when I was up north with my mother, in Kirkenes.

You're so down, I was *often* told. *Not so gloomy, Heinz, don't be so down.* That was something I had to make an effort to achieve. What I could do *well*, a role I felt at home in from the outset was August Keil, the poor devil in Hauptmann's *Rose Bernd*, who's suffering from lung disease. He's almost struck down by his antagonist. *Sickly* characters, that's what I was good at. Or loathsome, fascistoid types. They come from the *very* bottom, from the lowest, the lowest and most backwards. Like me. I was good at those roles. I played Spiegelberg in Schiller's *The Robbers*, Spiegelberg is another one. He finishes everything off. But then he's finished off. I played a lot of schemers who hound others to death and enjoy it.

And in *Rose Bernd*, that was an exception, there I played a weak man, August Keil. A fragile young man who's destroyed by Streckmann. Streckmann flattens his nose and punches one of his eyes out. Which then happened. At the premiere, the guy playing Streckmann hit me so hard that blood spurted all the way to the front row. The curtain falls after that scene and there's an intermission right after the punch in the nose. And I was stretched out unconscious on the stage. There was a doctor in the theatre who brought me back to life.

My nose was still broken in the second performance. And that Streckmann was just the same. Same thing again, from the top. And again and again. The theatre was not good for me. If you're unlucky and a play is well received, and *this* one was *very* well received, it's often difficult to survive it.

For August Keil, I didn't have to look for a model—I was that man. *Pale face, thinning hair and prone to occasional nervous twitching. He is skinny, narrow-chested and his entire appearance betrays a homebody* is how Gerhart Hauptmann describes him, as if he'd written the play with me in mind.

I was already losing my hair at nineteen. And my occasional nervous twitching didn't escape Hauptmann. My years of boozing left me with faint trembling that some people took for *nerves. Stop with the nerves*, Herbert often said, usually when he wanted to distract himself from his own nervousness. *Heinz, stop with the nerves.*

This role, August Keil, this man who was so afflicted, I grasped such characters best. I found myself in these people but onstage, while acting, I was always afraid. Because the actor came up to me, he came up to me as Streckmann and hit me full force in the face. He didn't like me and took it as a chance to make me pay for it. Every show was a settling of accounts. The character punches an eye out. The actor broke my nose. Repeatedly. He was one of those *Nazi actors* who never got over the fact that history didn't turn out in their favour. He was a *fighter pilot*, as they were called. He flew his plane *to England*. There he dropped his bombs and was proud of it, twenty years later he was still proud of what he did *for the Führer*.

Rose Bernd is twenty-two when her lover, a married man, gets her pregnant. My mother was twenty-two when Halbsleben got her pregnant. And for her, too, there was probably another man involved.

My mother was *engaged* to Halbsleben. And Rose Bernd was *pledged*, pledged against her will to *me*, to August Keil, who loves her and *overlooks, wants to overlook* everything she might have done, with a patience she will have a hard time escaping.

    Her father has promised her to this *narrow-chested, twitching homebody*. She's meant to marry this man and is pregnant with a married man's child. Streckmann, who'd been after her for years, although she never paid attention to him, discovers their secret affair and spreads rumours. It comes to a trial, during which she commits perjury. She's faced with jail. In spite of it all, August Keil stands by her. He appears absolute, almost ruthless in his love. In any case, there's no way out for Rose Bernd. She decides not to allow her child to be in this world and strangles the baby. *The child should stay where it belongs*.

My mother didn't strangle me with her hands. Even if against her will at the time, she gave me up, left me behind, abandoned me right after I was born. But she herself was also abandoned and discarded, chased away. Still, she then wanted to know if her Heinz was alive. She searched for me and tracked me down at the farmer's who daily burned himself in me with the question of *where* my mother was and why she didn't come to get me, to take me away. Maybe she had a guilty conscience when she was with her lover in Lindau or wherever else she might have been.

All I know is that in Hohenems there was my father, my *real* father, and he had a sister. He had a mother, too. It was Ingrid who told me, Ingrid was his daughter, my half-sister, *yes, Heinz, I know they didn't like your mother. That's why she left.* She told me this in so many words. And I was thankful that she was so honest. So, institution or no institution, my mother was gone, at least for me she was, the next four years she wasn't there. It did me good to hear my half-sister say that. I'd always wanted to know why my mother had had to leave so soon. All the way from Kirkenes, she lands in Hohenems and very soon after that she has to disappear.

There are some mothers—it's nothing new—mothers who *give up* their children and don't look for them and don't *want* to hear anything about their children. Later I also learnt from my half-sister in Hohenems that her grandmother, that is my allegedly *real* father's mother, my grandmother, had *despised* me. She'd hated *me* and had hated *my mother*. For that reason alone, I'd had no future in Hohenems. But my father never came. My mother believed he would come and marry her. That's why she was institutionalized the first time. Right after I was born, it was over for me.

    Whether it was actually *me*, I don't know either. She'd always said, *they switched you. You're not mine.* Could be. I was in a *home* at first, a home that some said wasn't *that kind* of home.

My father didn't come and then his mother got involved. Ingrid admitted it in tears. Because this *grandma*, this woman would have been my grandma; she'd hated me when I was just an infant. Then I landed in Lustenau. With that farmer.

    I should have lived with his mother while *he* was still at war, in Norway, that had been the plan, together my mother and I were meant to live with his mother. That's what my sister told me. This had *shocked* her. One day, she got in touch, *unfortunately* there was something she had to tell me. She had learnt from her father, that *his* mother, in other words *her grandmother*, had *wished us to hell*, my mother and me.

And then came the *long* period of time, during which there was nothing between my mother and me. Whatever the circumstances, she was gone and came back. Things could have turned out very differently for me with that farmer back then. He burned my mother into me. *Where's your mother from, where*. And now, when I think of it, when I think of her, I grab hold of the pinky finger of my left hand, that's the spot, our spot, and most of all, the burning, that *was* my mother. This pain is the first thing I learnt about my mother, from these people, out of whose mouths I heard the word *mother* for the first time. *Where's your mother from, where?* When *she* said to me, *I don't know, Heinz, are you the one or aren't you*, then I showed her the scar and she couldn't understand why I was showing it to her.

When she stood before me that time at the farmer's, a stranger who was supposed to be my mother and whose language I couldn't understand and who wasn't sure, *is he the one, or is he not*, she looked at me with doubt in her eyes and I stretched my arm out, held my finger out to her, the finger on which the man had *marked* me. I thought the scar would be the sign, would be evidence of where I came from. *I'm from there*, I said.

She bent down to me and looked into my eyes and took me with her, took me away from there.

At the beginning of our time together, I kept trying to find this sign on one of her hands, I looked at her hands often, very often, wanting to see a mark on one of her fingers that might have been branded on to her in the same way and by which we could recognize each other. But that's not how it was. She didn't have the sign. Maybe that was the source of her doubts, I thought. Nonetheless, she took me. She must also *believe* that I'm the one, that I'm Heinz.

And on top of everything, there was this Halbsleben who claimed I was the child *of a Russian who drowned*.

In the meantime, I *decided*: I'm half Norwegian and half Russian. If my actual *progenitor* claims that I'm not his son but the child of *a Russian who drowned*, then the truth is that I don't want to be *this man's* child.

My half-siblings didn't want to hear this, but it's not a made-up story. The usher in the theatre where I worked, Radtke or whatever his name was, a fine man, who was *also* born in Hohenems—when we got to know each other, we very soon also had a personal relationship, he said, *Heinz, you're not Halbsleben's son*. Why not? *Well, in Hohenems he's always saying that you're the child of a Russian who drowned*. That was burned into me so deeply that the Russian, the drowned Russian, is *closer* to me than Halbsleben. My half-siblings in Hohenems know this and they're ashamed of it. Because it's not made-up. This Rudolf Radtke, why would he tell a story like that. He was completely surprised. *No, you're not Halbsleben's*. I certainly am Halbsleben's son. *No*. And then again: *you're the child of a Russian who drowned. He always said that*.

All this is known. But it can't be said too often, because it got cemented inside me, it's my biography and in my head—it can't be *changed*. When the one who got my mother pregnant says that—I could never talk to her about it after all—then it can't be otherwise. Maybe she *did* have another relationship. Maybe he's not lying. Maybe he felt humiliated. Maybe that Russian *was shot* in the water, in which he supposedly *drowned*. In any case, the fact is that I now feel I'm half Russian and half Norwegian, naturally with the added insanity of my mother always repeating, *you're not mine*.

Time and again, I saw movies about *Lebensborn* and about these homes. In one of these movies I saw a room, a large room, a hall actually, and in the centre of this hall there was a table, an enormous table, and on this table there were dozens of—at first I thought they were rabbits hopping around the table—but on a closer look they were children, they were infants covered with powder rolling around on the tabletop. They'd been dusted with something, I can picture it now. This image froze inside me. They'd probably been dusted with some kind of powder. I can see a nurse. Surrounded by a cloud of powder. They were infants. And when my mother often claimed, *you're not mine, you were switched, you fell off the changing table back then*, she often said this and when I picture the little, wriggling bundles, I think it could be true.

And if it were true, *if* I had been switched in one of those powder clouds, then it wouldn't be any different from what is happening today, even now. How many children are there in Africa or in Syria now, in war zones everywhere, who are constantly being switched? The parents are locked up or shot or they die in a rubber boat out at sea. Small children sit on a beach or in ruins somewhere. *How* can they possibly know where they come from? How many children who were born up until 1942, like me, and even until '45 or '46, how many of these *Lebensborn children* are unaware of *who* they *are* or who they may have been? And now, now the children—they sit there, somewhere, and *doctors without borders* or whoever comes along and takes them somewhere else. And we'll never know how many of these children drown in the sea every day because they're fleeing from someplace. Fleeing somewhere. And in the meantime, the boats have been forbidden from rescuing these people. It's chilling. On every one of those boats and in every port, there should be a Grüninger who doesn't send these people back across the *Alter Rhein* from back in those days and now. The boats may be full, and they *are* full just like back then, but the ports are not.

How many young mothers brought their child into the world in a *Lebensborn home* and left them there, maybe had to leave them for whatever reason, and did *not* come back, the way my mother *did* come back for me, or they came back and didn't find their children, they found nothing at all. And how many left their children in the homes and then never looked for them and so never set in motion the children's search for their parents? Many of these children didn't have *the place* burned into them like I did, but *the search for that place* was burned into them, a *gangrene* that never, ever stops, not even when the place or the person appears to have been found and the search could end if their mother or father were actually found. Then the searching begins again, from the very start, because each time the only thing that can be discovered at first is the *scar*, this once open *wound* that did close in the years since then, like a door, an access that has shut from outside and from within and can only be unsealed by splitting open once again, there is no other way.

My mother never uttered a single word about why she had to leave me behind back then or why she never stopped searching for me. The words for this had, no doubt, gotten lost in the years when we had no contact or information about each other, or when she perhaps didn't want to hear a word about me. She never found these missing words again. And if she had found them again, she would never have *uttered* them.

At the *Alter Rhein*, as Heinz Hörvold, I filled in for Lex Barker. In Saarbrücken at the age of thirty-three, I played Tarzan again as Heinz Fritz. In those years at the *Alter Rhein*, I wasn't yet Heinz Fritz and wouldn't be for some time. Only the name *Heinz* has stuck to me from the start. Heinz. *Why am I called Heinz?* That was another topic my *mute mother* never wanted to talk about. Heinz. Heinrich. Heinrich Himmler. *Reichsführer-SS Heinrich Himmler.* He's the one who established *Lebensborn* and surely the person I'm named after. Many of the *Lebensborn children* were called *Heinz* after this *faithful Heinrich*. It was set up in 1935—and lasted until the end of the war—for women expecting children fathered by *Wehrmacht* soldiers and members of Himmler's *SS*. Because these *unplanned* children were rarely aborted, the mothers were supported by this *association* of the SS. So that these children wouldn't perish and would be at Germany's disposal. This is the reason these homes were built and why the mothers and their children or even the children alone, without their mothers were taken from the occupied territories and brought *to the Reich*, so they could get a hold of these children. It was *Lebensborn* that brought my mother with me in her belly from Norway down to Hohenems. *Lebensborn* was everywhere or was intended to be wherever there were these mothers and their children, that was the plan. And yet hardly anyone knew about it. It seemed that only those *affected* learnt about it, very few beyond them. That was the appearance in any case. These women's children, *children whose good blood was racially certified*, in their parlance, should not be lost *to the Führer* and *the German cause*, but instead brought to the homes as a supply of fresh blood, of the *SS's* new seed for the *Führer*. Not because the *Lebensborn* had any concern for the mothers' interests, but because they wanted the children for Germany.

These homes were always shrouded in secret so they gave rise to fantasies and rumours from the start. Later, there were repeated claims that these homes were *brothels, breeding centres, mating stations* for the *Aryan race*. This is false and wasn't their purpose. The homes were shelters for women who'd become pregnant and could not bring their child into the world where they lived for whatever reason. In Norway, these women were at risk because consorting with the *enemy* was considered treason, as in my mother's case.

Not once did the word *Lebensborn* ever cross my mother's lips. In Lustenau not a single member of my stepfather's family knew about it. And years later, decades later, my half-siblings in Hohenems had no idea about *Lebensborn* and certainly not that I was one of those now-grown *Lebensborn offspring*, who was now to be belatedly laid in his biological father's nest, as it seemed. They weren't aware that in Dracula's Reich this word was shunned like the cross or the stake that could be driven into this *spectre's* heart. This word was hidden in her suitcase and remained there until I found it on that scrap of paper.

We didn't know. That appalling sentence. And yet it's true. This time. It applies to us. It's all the more important for some to know now.

Many people were destroyed by this *Lebensborn story*. It destroyed my mother. And I, too, am essentially a dead man because of it, or one of the undead, in any case. It's a good thing, too, since I could only survive as one of the undead.

My father's tribe, my stepfather's tribe—they were bullies. He got it from his father, from my grandfather. There were incredible stories about him. He fell eleven meters from a pear tree, stood up and said, now I want a bacon sandwich. That's how he was. He just couldn't say the word *das*. For him *das* was—*des*. That's why he was called *Desser* as were all who were part of his family, who lived with him, under him, *in the shadow of the pear tree*. He was the first *Desser*. His son, my stepfather, was a *Desser*. I, too, wanted to be a *Desser*.

Until '57, my name was Hörvold. That was my mother's family name. I didn't belong and was stateless. *She* received citizenship through marriage, but *I* didn't. He hadn't adopted me after all. My name was Hörvold. Hers was Fritz. I still had her Norwegian name. I didn't get the document, my proof of citizenship, until 1957. Then I got the name. His name. And suddenly I belonged.

The chaplain who gave me the accordion had pulmonary disease. And Fritz did too. He was already ill when my mother met him. He died in my arms. In the end, he weighed just thirty kilos. He hung on tubes in bed. *Kill me, Heinz, kill me.* I would lift him, but I hardly had to lift him, he was so light. Then he would spit, he'd spit blood. I wanted to give him liquid to drink, from a feeding cup, but it wasn't possible, it simply wasn't possible any longer. Once a week, the doctor came by and gave him morphine, but he should have had morphine far more often. He was in such pain and the pain drove him insane. When you waste away like that, over years, you stop being normal. I see it in myself. When the pain is too strong, I have lapses, I tell myself things that even I find macabre. I do this to distract myself from the situation. I tell myself something *crazy* and the pain lessens. As long as you know you're doing it, it's fine. But he didn't know anymore.

At his burial, they spat at my mother—at the open grave—and said to her, *you let our brother starve.* An enormous family, twelve brothers and sisters, eleven of them surrounded her. I was afraid she might have a fit at any moment, but then they left and we stood there alone.

We made it home somehow. There were only two beds in the house. There was the marriage bed, actually, it was made from two beds, which my mother had separated. She put one of them in the front room, where my father slept. I dropped onto that bed, dead tired. There was a crib, an enormous crib, in which my half-siblings and I had slept as children. I'd stopped that and now slept on the floor, on a blanket. I was exhausted and slept in the bed my father had died in. I fell asleep and he came to me in a dream, sat on the edge of the bed, took my hand and said, *soon, you'll come too.*

    My mother calmed me down, which was necessary because I had to get up at four—at four in the morning I had to leave. Father was dead and there were my younger siblings, my mother was very ill, I had to take charge of the family and that meant *the factory.*

There were machines that embroidered fabric, wedding dresses, dress shirts, all that. Sixteen hours a day. At *two* there was a shift change. Then work until *ten*. At *ten*, the night shift came and worked until *six*. And again, from *six* until *two*. We adolescents worked days. The night-shift wasn't for us. And when possible, we worked on Saturdays. Sundays we also did *construction* here and there to earn a bit extra. These are *semi-skilled* jobs. They don't pay much.

The factory was *im Moos*. Ten machines. My friend Otto worked there too but was a few years ahead of me. Herbert was there as well. He took the new wares, collected them and brought them to the other factory on *Pontenstraße*, where I ended up later.

Lustenau was a centre of embroidery. The first embroidery factories were built there after the *First World War*. Almost every house had a small extension added to the back. You needed eleven, twelve meters space for a machine. So extensions were built and covered with tin roofs. That's where the machines were kept. The entire family embroidered. *Everyone* there had to work, no exceptions.

If you had one of these machines, you were somebody. They cost money. But they also brought in money. These machines are money mills, everyone said, they could make you rich. Some only had *half* a machine, two friends, one half each. Even they could live off it.

Deals were made in Switzerland, in Altstätten. The goods, the embroidered fabrics, went to Africa, to India, they were supplied to the entire world. Then overnight, in 1932, that was it for embroidery. At least for a time. From one day to the next, the orders stopped. But the debts remained. People had invested, had bought a machine, a fitter would come and it could take around two months to finish the installation of the machine. This cost a tremendous amount of money. And so many of the houses *burned down*. The Lustenauers were maligned as *kindlers*, they set their houses on fire, it was said. In an attempt to collect insurance. On *one* day at *one thirty*, one house was on fire. Within two and a half hours, eight houses were engulfed in flames. It was *the* chance for it all to burn down completely. The household goods were stored in a wagon at the neighbour's. That was the story at the time.

Most started as *Schiffli-Fädler* or *shuttle-threaders*. The machine needs shuttles, shuttles that guide the threads. Feeding thread into the machine was called *fädeln*. The girls did the post-embroidery, they had to correct the mistakes. Others had to cut the threads. They had shearers for that. The fabric was pulled over an edge, a steel edge, above it was a trimmer mechanism. The threads were made to stand upright with a suction apparatus, with a brush and a suction apparatus, then they were trimmed with extreme precision. They were unsettling machines.

My stepfather was also involved with embroidery. He and a friend owned *one* machine. I never knew him, that friend. I believe he was no longer alive when I moved in with Fritz. And the machine was gone too.

These machines were called *plauers*. They came from *Plauen* in East Germany and they ran. Soon they'll be one hundred years old but I wouldn't be surprised if a few of them were still running.

I embroidered on a *plauer*. The factory was in my neighbourhood, right on the other side of the meadow in front of our house. I left the house and crossed the meadow, that huge meadow, and there I was, in the factory. The place was called *im Moos*. The factory was also called *im Moos*. The man who owned it had about thirty machines. Ten were across the meadow, where I was, and he had twenty more in the centre of town. From *Moos*—after about a year—I switched to *Ponten* in the centre of Lustenau, at *Pontenstraße* there were twenty machines. And at some point, out of the blue, very early, I think it was in the late 1950s, he sold everything and left. No one knew where he went. A reticent man, no family, nothing. He'd taken it all over, not from his father, but from his grandfather, I believe, and he was by far the richest man in town. Sold it all and disappeared. A guy like Howard Hughes who lived on up on the hundredth floor and conducted his business there in the 1920s.

But work didn't end for me because of it. The machines ran well so workers were *welcome*.

After that I landed with Oskar Hämmerle. *A&O Hämmerle*. One of them was called Adolf, he'd been in a concentration camp and was already an old man—going on ninety—when I arrived. Adolf was in a camp, that I know. And his partner, Oskar, also suffered a great deal and he was also an old man. I believe that *he* had also been in a camp. I did embroidery for him.

There were eight machines, they each had four. Oskar liked me. When I had no money, he'd give me an advance. *Just work a few hours extra.*

And once, a storm came in across Lake Constance and blew the roof off our house. Roofs were still shingle then. So I went to see Oskar, I went to the factory with a few shingles in hand, and in his office, he was lying on a couch under a blanket. He woke up, opened his eyes and said, *Heinz, how much do you need?*

I thought, I'll never earn that much my entire life. He went to the safe and came back with a little envelope. I didn't have to sign anything. *You're a hardworking guy, you'll work it off.* And that's how it went.

I was a threader, a shuttle-threader. I learnt on machines that were *running*. I liked the work. I liked dealing with the machines. And the machines liked me, at least that's how I felt. And I liked working with them. I was impressed by all they could do. And so I wanted to know *how* they did it and most of all what they were made of—I was interested in the inner lives of these machines. I'm a machine, too, in dealing with them I became one or I'd always been one, in any case, when something needed to be done to any of them, I was there. If a machine malfunctioned, a fitter was called, and I was assigned to him and he showed me how to take the machines apart. Almost two and a half thousand parts. One Friday noon we turned the machine off. He undid the *first* three screws. *You've got to start here, so that you remember*, he said. Then he showed me how you place all the pieces you've unscrewed one next to the other in a line. And then in the reassembly, you start from the end and work your way to the beginning. That's the fundamental rule. If you don't follow it, everything's lost.

By Saturday afternoon, we'd put the machine back together again. Then came the big moment. When everything is reassembled, you put the belts back on the motor, run it through *one time*, a *single* rotation. The fitter said, if you feel the slightest resistance *brake*. I turned and turned, the belts spun through and through. And it ran.

The machines' inner life fascinated me. *My* inner life interested the doctors. When I was nineteen, they wanted to remove my stomach. It was all too much for me, blood was coming from everywhere. I thought that maybe Fritz was right when he said, *soon, you'll come too*.

I was a sickly child. But tough, too, and always a little tougher than sickly. Having that sense gave me strength. But I always had to pull myself together, I still do. Another child hanged himself because he couldn't fake it. I was a good faker. I only ever faked being healthy.

I always ran away from doctors. And yet, if it weren't for a few of them, I'd have been done for long ago. Back then, too, when I was nineteen and it was a question of removing my stomach there was a doctor who helped me. He liked me. When a doctor likes you, you've won half the battle. An internist, Doctor Hefel in Dornbirn. Walter Fenz, who did so much for me and whom I met in the embroidery factory, sent me to him. He did a thorough examination. One of his *colleagues* was also present, another doctor. I lay before them on the table, a surgical table, I lay before them as if on a dissecting table, both of them palpated and squeezed and tapped me and talked to each other over me, *yes, maybe surgery, there are no other options left*. But then surgery wasn't an option after all, my sick mother, my younger siblings, I had to be *at home*, I had to function, an operation was *out of the question*. Suddenly the doctor said, *he's so young, I'll think of something*.

Because of what he thought of, I was almost healthy for a time, that is, I was never *healthy* and the reason was: whoever was born in '42 had nothing to eat as a child. And there was my mother, a Norwegian, to begin with I was alone for years, everything was very meagre, and later, when my mother was back in my life, we still had nothing. There were those famous *care packages* from the Americans. Without those *care packages* we'd have gone crazy, my mother and I. No one gave us anything. There *were* farmers, there *were* people with animals around us, who probably had eggs or meat. But they didn't like her, *the Norwegian whore*. All there we got was *please get lost, get lost with that boy there. Go away.*

Later, as an embroiderer, as a *shuttle-threader* and *checker*, I did earn money. And yet, there was never enough to eat at home. I'll never forget, I was already sixteen, when my brother brought *half an apple* to the factory. *Half* an apple, even though the meadows were full of apples and pears and all kinds of things. But woe to you if you picked up an apple, the farmer would beat you half to death if you stepped foot on a field that wasn't yours. And in the neighbourhood, among my father's relatives, no one reacted, no one in the whole area. And there was my brother, seven years younger than me, with half an apple and a *rogge*, that's what they call a piece of black bread, with the crust of a rye roll. He handed it to me through the window. That was my meal. And it was *his* meal too.

I'll never forget this woman in the factory, her name was Mia. She always hid when she ate. She would pull a blanket over her head and sit there, eating her bread and butter under the blanket because she didn't want anyone to see her chew. I was in love with her. Because I liked the fact that she didn't want anyone to see her eat. I don't like it either.

I always dreaded *eating on stage*. It lifts some actors' spirits. Eating scenes on stage, no matter how well written they are—*another chicken cutlet and another piece of cake*—make me nervous. I don't like to *see* other people eating either. When I offer someone food, I don't want him to suffer because of it. I've been offered many things that made me suffer. That's why I prefer the privacy of home, it's the same as pulling a blanket over my head. Mia couldn't eat in her own home, she also worked double shifts, so she *had* to eat in the factory.

I imitated her. I covered myself, too. *What are you doing under the blanket? I'm not going to take it away from you.* But they *did* take it away from me, repeatedly. And from her, too, no doubt. There are people who don't want to let others eat. Just the way they *look* at you when you're eating is enough to give you a coughing fit.

I played that on stage, too. In Botho Strauß's play *Trilogy of Reunion*, an orgy of eating, my role was of someone who was constantly dropping things because he is so closely *watched*.

On the eve of an exhibition opening, a group of the curator's friends and acquaintances is invited to an art association and the character I played, his name is Felix, this *Felix* was also me in real life. At this dreadful party I meet Richard, a printer, whose memory has been going for some time and despite, or because of, this, he wants to tell me the story of a long novel he'd recently read. He actually manages to tell most of the story in all possible and impossible remembered variations, although now and again he's not sure *why* he wants to tell it to me or what it is that's he wants to communicate by telling it.

I listen to him attentively for a long time but after a while I stop listening and try to slip away. I'm constantly holding a slice of bread in my hand, a *roll, roast beef and mayonnaise*, as if I were trying to hold on to *something*.

The others in the group, too, are watching and eyeing each other suspiciously, talking at each other, but not *with* each other. They listen and sound each other out, on guard against each other and themselves. They stand before the pictures in the exhibition and walk back and forth and yet they have eyes and ears only for the stories of the people around them.

While Richard doesn't stop trying to force me into his trains of thought and constantly watches his effect on me, I gnaw at and chew on my *sandwich*. What he craves is having influence on others. What I crave is retreating. The more Richard senses that I'm *drifting away*, the more vehemently he presses me and drills into me because he correctly recognizes my *struggle with the sandwich* as the escape attempt it is. What I'd like most is not to stop at the sandwich, but to devour *myself* whole, to eat myself out of the situation and away from that place. But I keep dropping bits of the sandwich, the bread, the roast beef, the lettuce. I pick it up and keep eating, I try to keep eating, but let things fall again, out of clumsiness, embarrassment, or despair. Out of hatred. Perhaps also out of hatred. Because there's no evading the others' observation.

The mayonnaise drips down my shirt, onto my trousers. Embarrassed, I try to clean myself while my counterpart continues tormenting me so that there's no discreet way of dealing with the mess, not least because Richard is openly mocking my attempts to get a hold of myself. Yet no matter how hard I try to pay attention—the roast beef and the bread fall on the floor—I pick it up and don't know *what to do* with it. So I eat it, I choke it down, even though it doesn't get any smaller, until Richard finally loses the thread completely and starts to castigate me for not only failing to support him in his rendition, but also for trying to utterly disconcert him with my inexcusable behaviour.

It matters whether I'm seen *as an actor* and recognized on stage as the person I'm *portraying* and the person I *am* at that moment and for the appointed time or, in fact, as the person that I *seem* to be, at least to myself.

That's one reason I've always avoided opening night parties. What you've just *done* on stage isn't over, the effects last, you *consist* of it for an extended time. I always went home after the performances. Maybe because I wanted to get away from the character, to get out of the character, or maybe even because I *didn't* want out, because I couldn't disentangle myself from the person I'd just been. For me it was always significant that I'd found *a way* to the people I *portrayed* and who I *was* on stage, to whom *I* was entrusted, actually. I often found a way, but just as often I couldn't. But afterwards, the way returned to me. I simply left *after* a premiere, I'd leave *before* the opening night party and would sit in my room—I usually had just one room, I always lived in apartments—and I'd sit there, I'd sit by myself and have something to eat. *Without anyone watching.*

Mia was also like that. I appreciated that. We both had blankets over our heads, under which we ate our way towards each other. Sometimes, she'd slowly lift the blanket. I couldn't see but, I could feel her checking to see if I was keeping blanket over head, too. I was nineteen when *she* came to the factory, but she was—I liked her. And then, when it came to eating, or not *just* to eating, we had our very own corner, there were enough rolls of fabric that it was easy to hide, behind the rolls, but also under a blanket, each under our own.

The only one who didn't think this was strange was Walter Fenz, *the submariner* who sent me to Doctor Hefel and later wrote my letters of recommendation to acting school.

He was born in '25 and could have been my father. And in his way he was, for a time. I often spoke *pompelusisch* with him, a secret language made up of a lot of *laughter*. Very old people still understood *pompelusisch*, *he* understood it a little, *I* not at all, and so I fooled around with him as I probably only had with my mother in the days when I couldn't understand her. In Lustenau they even called my mother's *German pompelusisch* when they wanted to make fun of her.

Because he was there, this Walter, the hours in the factory passed more quickly. He was also the one who told me the story about the Hörmoser's, the old married couple with whom we lived in the early days, my mother and I, the ones who always helped us in the most difficult stretches but couldn't help themselves and died in a fire.

At seventeen, Walter volunteered to serve with the navy and was then stationed on a submarine. At some point they went too deep and for too long. That's what someone said, it didn't come from him, someone from the factory said that the sub had gone so deep that Walter never surfaced from those stories again.

He felt guilty. But he also remained a soldier. He never got rid of the soldier in him. But he was the one who spoke *pompelusisch* with me, who sent me to Doctor Hefel, and helped me in many other ways. I could always go to him.

I went to him. And I went to Christl Singer from Dornbirn. At fifteen I started at the first factory, *im Moos*. That's where I met her. Herbert introduced us, he knew her already. She worked in the big factory, on Pontenstraße. From there she came to us at *im Moos*.

She was seventeen, I was fifteen. She lived in Dornbirn, in Mühlebach. I still had an old bicycle, from my father, from Fritz, and I rode there on it. When it was broken, I walked through the fields, *overland*, and from Lustenau to Dornbin-Mühlebach it's far, you're almost at the mountains, it's so far.

I had to fight for every friendship. At least that's what I thought. With her I didn't even try at first. *You don't have a chance.* If you hear this constantly, you start to believe it.

Sometimes she came to me, I was proud of that. She had a moped and came from Dornbirn. I still lived at home and my mother called, very loud, from the front steps probably so the entire neighbourhood could hear, *Heinz, your girlfriend's here*.

Because of Christl, not only did the hours in the factory speed by, but also the days and years.

Wherever I was, she was too. Most often we went to the movies, to the cinema, whenever we could manage and no matter what was playing. The first kiss, my very first ever. *Gone With the Wind*. I'd seen the film, but I'd seen it *without her*. In it, Clark Gable bends Vivien Leigh backwards very low when kissing her. I did the same with Christl, or tried to, I bent Christl Singer over backwards the way Clark Gable bent Vivien Leigh. You're going to break my back, she said. You're going to break my back.

We also often went to *the Rohr*, on the *Alter Rhein*. The way there led past the *Landhaus*, a secluded inn that had served as a stopover, a hideout, for many refugees before the war and during the war. I didn't know. Neither of us had any idea even though my friend, the Capuchin, had frequently alluded to how good things were now, on the *Alter Rhein* and in general, because it hadn't always been like this. We can't be thankful enough, he often said, but only as if in passing and I never asked him about it.

He'd spoken of this inn and the *Gasthof Habsburg* in Hohenems. People in the inn had helped the refugees. From the *Gasthof Habsburg* they first went to the *Landhaus*. Then the Swiss came to the *Landhaus* and took away those who helped the refugees escape. The *Landhaus* was surrounded by fields along the country road and was a good first stop on the way to the border, it was only a few hundred meters from there to the *Alter Rhein*. It burned down after the war, long after.

The *Rohr* was not a regular crossing. It's a conduit, actually, that brought and still brings water from Switzerland to Lustenau.

Some of the refugees tried to cross on top of this conduit, on this pipe, the older ones who didn't want to go through the water. Everywhere else, you had to go through the water. In spring and fall, the water was ice cold.

Right at the *Rohr*, there was no border station. It was a wild crossing. There was a regular crossing nearby, called *Schmitter*. And a bit further south, *Wiesenrain*.

Then, many years after I was there with Christl, it became a bathing area, all of Lustenau swam there. My friend Otto always said, the water's as warm as urine, that's how full it was there after the war.

But back then it was wilderness. The *HIGA men* kept having to cut down trees to maintain a good view of the border. The *HIGA men* were generally older men or men who had returned from the front, men that were needed *locally*. The *Border Protection Assistants*. In Hohenems, the inn they were housed in was the *Gasthof Post*. They were the ones who weren't fighting in the war, either because they had large families or because they were too old for the front. They surveilled and guarded the *Alter Rhein* and watched that particular spot on the *Rohr* especially strictly. Small structures were built section after section, in which they could shelter from the rain or warm themselves in winter.

The refugees were sent from the *Gasthof Habsburg* to the *Landhaus*. Those who helped them flee came from Switzerland to the *Landhaus*, they crossed the border and collected them there. Often, they were paid refugee smugglers who later stood trial and were sentenced in Switzerland.

The municipalities on the Swiss side, Widnau, Diepoldsau, and Au, these are neighbouring municipalities of Lustenau and in the Middle Ages they were part of the *Reichshof Lustenau*. But around the year 1600, the Rhein was set as the border and from then on, they were Swiss. But their territories were still on the Lustenau side, the *upper* and *lower Swiss marshes*. The fields are still there and still belong to the Swiss. Because they had to cultivate these plots during the war, they could cross the border to the Austrian side and many of them took advantage of this to do some trading or to serve as a contact in Switzerland. They claimed they had to till their fields and so were allowed to cross the border. They drove their carts back and forth and would often hide someone in the hay or smuggle them across some other way.

Christl Singer was the first one I swam across the border to Switzerland with. After her, there wasn't a second person for *that*. We had our camp next to the *Hansel-and-Gretel tree*, we studied maps near the *ant tree* and listened to the wind beat the driftwood against it. Wherever I went, Christl Singer went too. Through her I was *whole* for the first time. With her I was *whole*. Until then everything about me was *half*. A half-brother. With a half-sister. A *step*father and a mother who said I wasn't hers.

In the years with Christl, from fifteen to twenty-three, when I worked in the factory, in the embroidery works, during that time, I was *whole*.

And then it ended. At twenty-three I went to acting school in Wiesbaden. I wanted her to come with me, but she didn't want to. We wrote each other a few times. Then she wrote that she was married and we stopped writing. We saw each other once more. Then I got a letter saying that we'd been seen together and could we please never see each other again.

I *immortalized* her twice on stage, even if only for the duration of the performance each time. Once as a bank manager in a Peter Turrini play, *Love in Madagascar*. And again in *Piaf*, in the play *Piaf*. I played an American bartender. Both characters, the manager and the bartender, recount a lost love. In both plays, the love's name wasn't given, so I thought that I could give the women a name.

Love in Madagascar. The owner of a run-down cinema comes into my bank and wants a loan to go to Cannes and make another and final movie with Klaus Kinski. Kinski is on his deathbed, but the man doesn't know this. He's hopelessly in debt and desperately needs the loan. I, as manager, tell him about my first love and how, when I was sixteen, I experienced the *most beautiful moments of my life* in his cinema with a student in the other class in our grade. Just as *I, myself* had. It all applied to me, too. With Christl Singer, I was always in the cinema and also had my *most beautiful* moments there.

But in the play, this story didn't give any name. And so I gave it one by talking about Christl Singer.

In *Piaf*, I was an American bartender. Édith Piaf once gave a guest performance in America, but it went badly. And in the play, there's a scene with a bartender who also wept over a lost love. And, I said, here again we don't have a name, what's she called then?

Well, this time say *Chris, Chris Singer*.

Naturally it didn't always work, but now and again it did. Then I simply said, *Christl Singer,* as if for no reason and seemingly pointlessly I said, *Christl Singer*. Or called her name. The way my mother had shouted from the front steps so the entire neighbourhood could hear, that's how I called her name from the stage into the audience. Maybe she's sitting in the theatre, I thought, or someone who knows her or might possibly have known her and will tell her that somewhere in the world, even if only in a play, someone is thinking of her.

Herbert brought us together, Christl Singer and me. I owe my first love to him. I also owe him my friendship with his father.

Franz Jäger was an Alpine dairy farmer and to reach him, you had to pass through the *Rappenloch gorge*. You reach it from Dornbirn. And then, after a ways, you get to a *Vorsäß*, which is what they call an Alpine foothill, and from there you climb to the larger pastures higher up. You can go to the *Vorsäß* as early as May, even if there's snow at higher elevations. Entire families would move up there to work and live. He made cheese up there, and butter. They would usually stay all of May on the *Vorsäß* until mid-June, depending on the weather conditions and when the meadows were completely grazed, they'd move up to *Obergüntenstall*. That's a well-known Alp. *Obergüntenstall* is very high up and you can see it from Lustenau, a large mound, you can recognize it by the mound. I stayed up there with him as long and as often as I could. Even as a child, I'd be up at the hut with Franz in summer, with Erwin and especially with Herbert, but often with just Franz alone too. He was often up there alone, but I did see his wife up there too. They'd stay up there from June or July until September, until around the end of September. They could also go down to the foothill, to the *Vorsäß* when there was snow higher up. They stayed up there for about two months and in September, late September there was a certain day, usually about the 27th, when they either went straight down to the valley or back up to the *Vorsäß* one last time if enough grass had grown in the meantime.

The trek up to Franz Jäger was an adventure each time because even if no one admitted it, everyone was afraid of the gorge. And of the bridge, the *Rappenloch bridge*. If I was making the trek *alone*, I sang the songs he taught me to myself. If someone was with me, together we'd laugh the fear from our souls. We all had respect for the *Rappenloch gorge* and the *Rappenloch bridge*. All of us except Erwin. He was the only one who wasn't afraid of it; he wasn't afraid of anyone or anything, at least that's how it seemed to me. And it was Erwin who jumped off that bridge. It was the 31st, New Year's Eve, Herbert sent me a telegram. And a few days later, very soon after, another telegram came from Herbert. His brother had hanged himself.

I can still see Erwin running back and forth across that bare bridge, his eyes wide and his arms outstretched, he ran across that bridge like a wild man. Each time, I couldn't breathe. If I had jumped off it, if *I* had hanged myself, it would have been natural. Completely natural. But I always did it wrong. There are people who don't do those things right. I'm one of them.

I only liked the mountains when I was up high with Herbert's father, with Franz on his mountain. You could only spend time with him in the mountains. Still, despite all the surrounding mountains, I felt *at home* there with him, because he hadn't said anything to me about *hanging* yet. That came later, I was around sixteen, just before he took me down to my father's; it was the time when I had those panic attacks when Dracula came to me daily and all I did was bleed, internally and externally, and he said to me out of the blue, suddenly and without warning, he said right to my face. *Heinz, you'll hang yourself. Your uncle did it and you'll do it too.* I carried that around with me for a long time. I already had one *attempt* behind me, when I tried to split my head open at twelve. *When one person in a family hangs himself, then a second one does too*, he said.

Franz Jäger came from Hohenems. In the First World War, he was caught in an avalanche, somewhere in Italy, and a young man found him in a mass of snow after a long time. The young man dug him out and there was a lot that was wrong with Franz Jäger after that, a whole lot. That's how Franz himself told the story. It was Christmas time when the avalanche happened. Around that season, he always cried. At Christmas, he cried and talked about that time. I listened to him, I was the only one who did, no one else wanted to hear his stories. I was the only one who listened. I couldn't get enough of his stories and talking in general. At home, there was only silence.

I liked the mountains only until he made his remark about *hanging*. After he said it, from then on, my relationship with him was broken. I remember that Milli, Herbert's mother, was there. She was a marvellous singer, Milli was, and she said to him, come now, don't say a thing like that to him. But it was said. For years it was like a vaccine, I really thought that I'd hang myself, that one day it would come to that.

When I told my half-sister, Halbsleben's daughter, forty years later, more than forty years later—before that I didn't know she existed— I asked her about my uncle's suicide. She was furious. It's not true, no one in our family hanged himself. You don't even have an uncle. With Ingrid, I never know what's true and what isn't. With the whole family, I don't know what's true.

I didn't trust him an inch after that. And yet he's the one who took me to my father. I was sixteen when he told me, *I'm from Hohenems and I know your father*.

And once, I was with him again at the hut, the animals were fed, we were sitting in the room and had made ourselves comfortable. He lit a candle and I thought he would start singing one of his songs, but he blew out the candle and asked into the darkness: Your father, your *real* father, don't you want to meet him? Now that Fritz is dead, there's no obstacle. And I said, yes, if he's alive. Is he? I asked.

And how, he is. I know him. And I think it's time you met him.

The very next day we were down in the valley, on the way to the realm of my *bodily* father. I already had my moped by then, a *Sissy-Roller*, just like Christl Singer had. He sat behind me and tapped which direction I should turn with his fingers. In Hohenems, he suddenly leaned closer in to me and said, we just passed the house, you can reconsider. I pretended I hadn't heard him and he directed me to the train station. There we stopped.

My mother had arrived at this train station when she came down from Norway. That's what was written in the *Lebensborn itinerary*. *Bahnhof Hohenems* was the final stop on her trip from Kirkenes, that is, it *should* have been the final stop, if her wrong-way drive through the rest of her life hadn't begun right there. She arrived in this town and was supposed to be met at the station. And there I was, at the very same spot with my friend, whom I'd known for so many years and who already knew my father, my *real* father at a time when he couldn't have known my mother yet, when I hadn't been born yet, when not even my mother had been born yet, he knew my father.

Why is he telling me all this *now*, I thought, *why only now*? And that I would kill myself, why did he say that?

No one came to collect my mother, at least not in the way she had imagined they would in Norway. And so *he*, Franz, had come to collect me, now, sixteen years later, to lead me into the story with my father, a story that could perhaps have begun this way. But perhaps it was all very different, actually, because the fact that he knew my father didn't mean that all this time he *knew* that this man to whom he was leading me was my father. He only said, *I know your father, he's from Hohenems, like me*. He didn't say more than that.

At an inn on Kaiser-Franz-Josef-Straße, he signalled to me to stop, and while I sat on the *Sissy-Roller* for a time, he paced back and forth in front of the inn, telling me about people I'd never heard of before, which made me realize how little I'd known about him over all these years, because even though he had told and taught me so much, he'd never mentioned these kinds of stories.

During the war, a homeopathic doctor had had a practice, a man from Luxemburg, he said. He was a good practitioner and well liked. People came here from all over, his waiting room was always full. The patients waiting fell into conversation and these conversations also concerned the war. At the time, the first bombs were falling on the area. Once a woman came from Bregenz, a businesswoman who had spoken with another woman in this waiting room about how terrible it was that there were such bombing raids. She even said that the war was the Germans' own fault, and so was the fact that these bombs were falling here on our region and elsewhere, for that matter. It's the Germans' fault and they're even dropping bombs themselves, in fact, maybe the bombs that are falling from the sky on us here are German bombs.

I couldn't figure out why he was telling me this story or what he was trying to communicate with it, now that we were supposedly on the way to see my father.

One of the women in this waiting room reported this and denounced her. The *Gestapo* took the woman who'd made the comments into custody. In Bregenz, in the old city. She was released because of illness, but then they arrested and imprisoned her again later. She was beheaded in Vienna on charges of sedition. She died because of her comments, he said. And it happened here, in this building.

I cupped my hands around my eyes to see inside better. But he pointed to the building on the other side of the street that was reflected in the windowpane, the building to our backs, which I hadn't even noticed. He didn't point directly at the building but tapped his finger on the reflection in the tavern's window.

It's the building across from us, he said. That's where he lives.

What should I do? I asked.

It's a butcher shop. Go in and buy a couple of sausages. Then you'll see.

I turned and crossed the street. Only now did I really look at the building. It was larger than the others nearby. He was right, it was a butcher shop. The entrance faced the street. I climbed the steps and went in. Across from the door was a glass fronted counter. In the display case were sausages and cuts of meat of various sizes. On the counter was a large glass jar of pickles.

Behind the counter, a woman cut thin slices from a thick sausage on a slicer and laid them on a piece paper. She did this carefully and as if engrossed in thought, one at a time, piece by piece, she laid the slices on the paper and then all of it on a plate, which she placed next to full plates and platters in the display case. When she was done, she looked up. At that moment, a door behind her opened and a man came into the room, carrying two large cuts of meat on his shoulders, they stuck out like wings. He stood before me like a giant bird. He looked at me and froze, at least that's how it seemed to me, he loomed before me with those clumsy wings raised and outspread. There he was before me, the man who had appeared so often in my imagination when the ceiling would open up and he would come at my throat and start talking about my mother, only to end up asking me about her each time. I'd finally found him, here in his castle, in this butcher shop, on his way from the slaughtering room to the refrigerated room. I'd tracked him down in his hiding place. It was broad daylight. He wouldn't crumble to ash all that quickly, I knew this, too, now.

I looked at him and saw that he was looking at me. He *had* to have recognized me. I was blond. Like my mother. Platinum blond. You couldn't miss it. There weren't many blondes in the region at the time. And he knew I was living in Lustenau.

He gave me a penetrating look, an inquiring look, actually reluctant, he stared at me for a while. But his next movement was to swing towards me, I was in the way, I was used to standing in the way, he stopped, looked at me and kept going, that is, he went right through me, without facing any resistance, he went through me as if I weren't there, right in his way, as if I weren't there at all, he went through me and without turning around, I could see how he bent down behind me, after abandoning me yet again, how he bent down and rose up, and then, with his sides of pork wings beating wildly, he disappeared.

He was gone. But I was still there. And the woman was still there, smiling sweetly at me. She handed me a few sausages wrapped in paper—which I hadn't ordered. With wooden tongs, she fished a pickle out of the oversized jar and held it out to me over the counter, and with that I left my father's castle, went down the steps and crossed the street where my friend was sitting on the moped, waiting for me.

The next time I ran into Anton Halbsleben, I was sixty years old. Before he was against it. After I met him in his butcher shop, I wrote him. Then a letter arrived. Not from him, from his lawyer. I was to leave him in peace *or measures would be taken*. My half-sister didn't want to hear about it, forty years later. But I did receive that letter. I was sixteen years old. I mentioned it to her—do you know about the letter? Of course not. I wrote that I would like to meet him. Then that letter came. And then nothing more. Until I was sixty, that was it for the two of us.

After some time, I told my mother about the meeting. She was terrifyingly furious. She told me to leave him in peace—did I not understand that he didn't want to have anything to do with me?

I said that yes, I understood. Nevertheless, I'd wanted to see him once.

She did, too, she'd wanted to see him once. And it never happened. They'd agreed to meet. In Dornbirn. In the *Rote Haus*. She waited there alone, and no one came. For her that was it, for her it was finally over.

I thought that now, after Fritz's death—Fritz, who only ever humiliated her—she would come alive as I did, as we all did. But it didn't happen. For a time, she was completely mute. Only gradually did she start speaking again, but in Norwegian, and because there wasn't anyone around who could understand her, she started *talking to herself* again. She'd done this earlier, she'd always murmured to herself barely audibly and nearly incessantly. As a child, I'd often wondered what the whispering meant; I thought they might be curses with which she covered everything around her. More and more often, I found her talking to herself. These were intense and contentious discussions; she would change her voice and manner, as well as the volume, as if she were arguing with someone who was trying to persuade her of something she had to resist emphatically. And in all the years I was consciously aware of my mother, she'd never smiled or laughed as much as she did during this period. She would burst into sudden and unexpected laughter, so loud that I was regularly startled. My siblings and I ignored this laughter because it often had a threatening aspect that we didn't want to provoke. I didn't know how to react. She answered all my questions with silence, or she already lay on the floor before a question could be asked. So I never learnt how to ask *in the right way* and couldn't begin at that point—I didn't have the courage.

There was no one she could communicate with in this way, so she talked or laughed to herself or about herself, I thought, and when she returned *to us* after these *foreign conversations*, she was even quieter than usual, more remote, too. Then she would smile to herself again, for hours, but as if she were up to something, as if preparing something she didn't want to reveal to us yet, for whatever reason.

Abroad, my mother was also completely on her own. She had not been at home back where she came from for a very long time. And yet, one day I thought, how would it be if she did try again with her Norwegian family and maybe she wanted to take us, her children, with her. It wasn't impossible and I wasn't entirely wrong in my assumption because soon after she took my siblings *on the journey*.

Her family had disowned her because she'd been involved with a German. And now she wanted to go back. She had no contact with her family. Or hardly any. Now and again a letter came from her older sister, from Aunt Jördis, but otherwise, *if* anything came from Norway over all the years, it was death notices, one after another, year after year.

They'd chased her away. That's the version that had become fixed in me. There was no sign that the situation had changed and yet, in her thoughts, she was already *on the way*, as I had been *on the way* for years when I swam across the *Alter Rhein*, without telling her. For years I'd planned to return with her where she'd come from, where we'd actually *both* come from. But in the meantime, these plans had ceded to other considerations—I was in the factory and in the process of settling in where I was.

As for her, she was determined to take this journey. Maybe she also wanted some kind of resolution with her family. That's probably why it was so important to her to have my younger siblings with her, as *proof* that she'd set down roots elsewhere or at least to give the impression that she had. In any case, that's how I saw it because she hadn't shared her travel plans with *me*, who was, after all, the reason that she'd had to leave. Nor did she talk of me accompanying her on the trip. She gave no explanations, it simply had to happen, otherwise something *would* happen to her and to all of us.

One evening—I'd just come home from work—she was waiting for me on the front steps, as she did every other day and yet something was different. And she didn't come into the house with me as she always did after finishing her cigarette.

In the kitchen, my siblings were packing. My brother wanted to take his football but it wouldn't fit into the suitcase and he wasn't going to go without it, absolutely not. They sat next to their small suitcases talking excitedly with each other. In Norwegian. When I asked what was going on, my sister lobbed a Norwegian word at me—which she'd never done before—then another and another, and my brother, who saw how much this upset me, explained that they were going to Norway for a while.

How long they were up there, I can't remember, nor can I remember *who* brought them back; she was no longer in a state to travel all the way from up there down here. However it happened, she came back from Norway and was *completely* insane.

How often she was in the *Valduna* clinic? Often enough since simply through her fear of it, she was there. Everyone with a nervous condition, with *mental illness*, ended up there, stroke victims or epileptics.

It was a former cloister that had been converted to a clinic. That's where my mother went each time. It looks different now. And it surely is different there now. Entirely modified, torn down and rebuilt. But that fort-like cloister, the building alone was terrifying at the time.

In part, it was part *charitable hospital* and part *mental asylum*. Sometimes patients went from the *charitable hospital* to the *mental asylum* and, when their condition improved, from the *mental asylum* to the *charitable hospital*. When exactly my mother was there or how often—I only know that we children were always afraid that she'd be taken away from us. And this fear was always called *Valduna*.

Valduna open up the door, his mother's coming back for more, she'll lie down in the first free bed and call herself cracked in the head.
That's what the children yelled at me on the way to school.

Early on, when she'd just come down from Norway, right after I was born in 1942, when we were separated and she disappeared for a few years, she mostly likely wasn't in *Valduna* because a year earlier the *psychiatric ward* had been cleared to make room for a military hospital. But until then they kept patients there. *Valduna* was the centre. People were rounded up from all over and kept there like animals.

One man in particular, a psychiatrist, Doctor Josef Vonbun, had them all dispatched. He had his own daughter killed with an *injection*. She was handicapped, a young girl. Doctor Vonbun was the director of the asylum. He drove his own car around the Bregenz Forest to visit old people's homes and poor houses and he took those he *selected* away then and there.

The patients were deported to Tyrol, to the local *insane asylum*, and from there on to Hartheim. In Hartheim, they were gassed. Or they were taken directly from *Valduna* to Hartheim. Around 600 people were taken from *Valduna* in this way and around 300 were murdered.

Anyone who tried to get someone out of these asylums was successful. If someone objected, people were saved. Saying nothing could be done is just an excuse. In Altach there was a mayor, a Nazi, but he was a friendly man and he helped a woman get her sister out of the asylum in Hall, so she wasn't murdered. Or Müller, the medical officer in Feldkirch, he also helped get people out again and again.

And my mother, there's *one time* when she was probably there. I was lying on the floor in the kitchen, too. Then a psychiatrist came with a doctor I liked, Doctor Gunz. I'm not sure how old I was, in any case I was already working in the embroidery factory. My younger brother had run and fetch this Doctor Gunz. He liked my mother. He helped her and often helped me, too. She lay next to me, twitching. Then the psychiatrist asked, *should we take him too?*

No, he stays here, he's stable. If Doctor Gunz had given a different answer, who knows, maybe I'd be in that asylum today. The sentences have been scored into me. *He's stable, we're not taking him*, he said and gave me an injection, in my stomach. That calmed. Then he asked if I could pack something for my mother, *something for her to take with her*. I looked and looked and finally found a jacket somewhere. My mother looked crazier than usual, it was a white jacket, from Norway, from the war, a fur coat, but not fur, just a thick winter coat. It was the middle of summer. They put it on her.

I believe I stayed in the kitchen. They left with her and she kept looking back at me as they walked to the car. It was just a few steps, and I can still hear her one sentence, *I don't want to lose my children, I don't want to lose my children*. She repeated it over and over.

During my time in acting school, I worked as an orderly and saw this kind of distress. The last woman I took care of had five children. A car accident. Her husband was on the floor above her. There was only *one* place on her body where I could take her pulse. And one spot on her mouth. Not a single part of this woman was unhurt. And she kept asking *are you taking care of my children, are you taking care of my children*, she kept asking me. How was I supposed to do that? How could I take care of her five small children?

I don't want to lose my children. I kept hearing my mother's sentence from this woman's mouth. That's why my mother often toyed with the thought of killing us three children. Because she had no one who take care of us if something happened to her.

She was picked up in an ambulance. That was the first dramatic stay. But there was definitely a second one, after she came back from Norway, after she'd been in Kirkenes with my *brother and sister*. Not long after that my brother came to the factory and told me I had to do something: *things aren't right with Mother*. When we got home, she was standing on the window sill on the second floor, talking to her Norwegian family, who seem to have rejected her yet again.

This time I took her to the asylum; we went there together.

What happened then, I found her *medical report* not long ago, used as a *bookmark* in a collection of Karl Valentin's stories of robber knights, it was a life mark, actually. Since then, I always have it with me.

<u>Patient name</u>: Fritz, Gerda
<u>Page number</u>: 1
<u>Admission number</u>: 15913 / 90 / 64

22.2.1964. Arrives at 14.30 in taxi accompanied by her oldest son to be admitted as a psych. patient.

<u>Hospital referral</u>: *Dr. Ludwig Gunz, Lustenau. Epilept. Dazed? Schizophrenia. Frequent attacks in recent days, tonight highly agitated, confused speech.*

Admission: Well-nourished, solidly built 45-year-old patient. Skin and visible mucous membranes evidence good circulation. Pulse 130/. Temperature not elevated. Lungs no findings. Patient makes a rather fractious impression, immediately says you're not going to kill me, are you? Answers questions promptly. Explains that she arrived in Austria in 1942, comes from Kirkenes, repeatedly emphasizes that she's clearheaded, but people say she's crazy. She was here once before at Christmastime, 3–4 days at most. Today's date is 17.3.1946.

Personal details of accompanying son: He is the oldest son and the only child of his mother and the father who brought pat. to Austria in 1942. There was no marriage because all of the father's relatives were opposed to pat. The pat. was not allowed to return to Kirkenes because she'd been outcast for travelling to Austria with a German soldier. Only last year was she allowed to visit relatives in Kirkenes. The adm. esteems his mother greatly for always keeping him with her, even though she had several opportunities to give him up. In 1946 she married another man with whom she has a reasonably good relationship, despite the fact that his relatives were hostile to pat. and the man himself often paid heed to the malicious talk of strangers and often beat her. This stepfather died four years ago and now she leads the household alone. She frequently suffers strong bouts of homesickness and at such time drinks wine or beer. She doesn't need to drink very much, a glass of wine is enough to make her intoxicated. Yesterday morning she started speaking confusedly, now Norwegian, now German. She believed her mother was still alive. Because pat. was loud and agitated, she was given Truxal for the night.

23.2 Became loud again early in the morning, speaking all manner of nonsense. Was given Truxal again.

24.2. *Personal details of patient*: She is a widow, born in Kirkenes. From her distracted speech it is evident that she suffers visual and aural hallucinations. She sees apparitions, hears her daughter in the corridor, suddenly says: 'You can talk nonsense with me,' speaks disconnectedly 'she's playing along,' looks at the ceiling and shouts: 'Don't laugh, Hannelore,' 'I see images,' 'You're all so beautiful.' Has menses. Says she is 45 years old, born in 1919. Did not give birth date, she is too distracted. Talks about light bulbs. Says it's not true that she wasn't a respectable girl. She can tell by the laughter and behaviour of others that they assume she wasn't.

<u>Conclusion</u>: Schizophrenia? Epilepsy.
<u>Treatment</u>: EST begun.

4.3. Improvement after the first 2 EST, agrees that this treatment is helpful. Calm, less disordered than before, but still not free of illness. Lies in bed. Shock treatment continues.

13.3. The improvement following the initial treatments (EST) did not last. Pat. is distracted, very absent at times, can only sleep with medication, yet is still calmer than before.

22.3. Weak epileptic attack during son's visit. Only now do we learn that pat. has had these attacks for 20 years, earlier in the month she had severe repeated attacks.
Before admission she also suffered frequent attacks and arrived in a dazed state. Electroshocks were suspended.

31.3. Fractious mood has lessened. With dosage of 3x1 Epilan no further epileptic attacks were observed.

<u>Summary</u>: Mrs. Gerda Fritz, born 1919, was in in-patient observation and treatment from 22.2–9.4.1964. Admitted in a confused and not entirely lucid state, staff failed to take an external medical history. Only later did we learn that pat. has been suffering from epilepsy for 20 years, which the subsequent fractious moods and excitability as well as the severe attacks have confirmed. We have put her on Epilan and with it have achieved some improvement.

Pat. was discharged on her insistence. Her son was convinced of the importance for her of following course of medication.

<u>Diagnosis</u>: Epilepsy.

And then came the moment when I was *upstairs* with her in the asylum and I shook her. Suddenly she opened her eyes and said, *Heinz, you have to become an actor.* She'd always said: *You have to get away from here and become an actor.* Nurses and a doctor and *yet another* doctor were standing around her, around her bed and they were absolutely astonished that my mother woke. She'd been in a coma. I shook her. And she opened her eyes.

And then I went *home*. And went back to see her. Again and again. And I spoke to a doctor. *Yes, it looks like you can come and take her home.*

What do you want to wear when I come to get you?
Bring the blue dress, she said.

To get to *Valduna*, you go from Rankweil into a valley. The train goes from Feldkirch to Rankweil. There's a station on the way, it's called *Amberg*. A forest road leads from *Valduna* to this station and it was said that when people, the patients, were taken away from *Valduna*, they were brought to the station along this road.

The first man says, I haven't seen you for a year and now you're so pale, where were you?

The second replies, I was in *Valduna*.

You shouldn't say *in Valduna*, the first replies, say you were in *America*. It sounds better.

Then he asks a third, well, where were you all year?

In America.

You were in America? How did you get there?

I took the train to Rankweil and from there took the bus back behind.

From there, back behind the station, I went to get her. It was a warm spring day and my route passed *through the villages.*

From Lustenau—usually I left straight from the factory when I went to see her—from there I continued via Götzis to Klaus and on through the *Vorderland*. Weiler, Röthis, Rankweil. *Valduna* is off the beaten track and so this was the obvious way, the most direct way, actually. A charming area, a protected area, the fruit trees bloom earlier there than in the rest of the country. And then the route reaches a river, the Frutz. Rankweil begins *after* the Frutz. For me, that's where the actual *Valduna region* begins, but we were all part of it, the entire countryside was *Valduna region*.

Via Rankweil, which was dominated by that church, the Church of Our Lady on the mountain of the same name, the *Liebfrauenberg*. And just past it, past the *Liebfrauenberg*, came the turn uphill to *Valduna*.

I brought her home from there. We followed the same route in reverse. She sat behind me on the moped in her blue dress, waving at everyone she saw as if she'd gotten to know them during her time in the asylum. From *America*, we went straight to Rankweil and in Rankweil to that mountain, the *Liebfrauenberg*. Like *Valduna*, the Church of Our Lady also resembled a fortress. And she wanted to see it, it was the first time my mother wanted to go in a church with me. We climbed a steep, winding path up the mountain. From the top we looked out over the surrounding land. The church was a prominent fixture on the way to *Valduna*. Rankweil *is* this church. When people think of Rankweil, they think of the *Church of Our Lady* and of *Valduna* right *behind* Rankweil. That was the phrase: *back behind Rankweil*. Every child knew what it meant.

In the church there's a miracle-working cross and a prayer stone on which you can kneel and make a wish. According to legend, Saint Fridolin was in some distress and had turned to God while kneeling on the stone, which then turned to wax and Fridolin sank into it. His supplication was heard and he was given the counsel and help he had prayed for. Since then, the faithful kneel on this stone and pray to have some request granted.

For a while, I had the feeling she would drop to her knees, but she didn't and we rode on through the villages. We stopped regularly and ran into the fields like children. Finally we reached a small rise to a chapel right next to the road. *Arbogast*. I'd often stopped to rest there on my return trips from the asylum, and I stopped there with her this time, too.

Arbogast. This is another famous pilgrimage site. The chapel's walls are covered with votive plaques with thanks for answered prayers. We walked up and down along these walls, reading our way from one story of illness and one expression of thanks to the next. Next to the chapel's external wall was a large stone, a prayer stone like the *Fridolin stone* in the *Church of Our Lady*. You could also kneel *into* this stone in order to become healed, body and soul and above all, to request a husband or wife. This time my mother did sit on the stone, not to pray for anything but out of relief; both of us now thought things would be better. In any case, I saw her there, sitting on the stone and thought of Saint Arbogast. *Saint Arbogast, send me what you can, be he stout or thin, so long as he's a man.* I whispered the saying into her ear. She nodded several times, then shook her head, and met my eyes with a laugh. I nodded and laughed with her since we were likely both thinking of Fritz. And I thought of Halbsleben, too. She hadn't been smothered by either of them. That was certainly worthy of thanks.

Many years later, there was another trip to Norway and this time I went along. My mother happened to be with me in Saarbrücken when her sister-in-law called and said, *if you want to come, come soon, we're not getting any younger.* She'd called because of an uncle who was severely ill and wanted to see her again. *So come quickly.*

My mother was happy. She felt that she'd been invited, which she had; they'd formally contacted her and asked her to come. She took it as an occasion to try again with her family and this time with me accompanying her.

I bought a car, an old *Opel Rekord*. I offered to drive her. My mother needed a seat and a half and sat in the middle of the back seat. That way I had her in sight the entire time, in the rear-view mirror. Off we went. Germany, Denmark, Sweden, Norway. When we drove through Sweden, it was on the *eastern* side, through the many birch forests, all such thin trees. She sat in the back and kept saying, *what matchsticks, what matchsticks*. She was *so* happy. Until the moment, when she *wasn't* doing well. Then we had to stop and find somewhere to stay.

I can see us driving north on those *endlessly* long roads, *Sweden*, and then a long stretch of Norway. Finland. In that extreme midnight sun. We didn't get tired and my mother became more and more talkative the farther north we were and the more she started telling me—more than she ever had before or would afterwards, excitedly, kind of insanely, actually, everything at once, muddled, and yet clearer than ever. And then, on the last stretch of the trip, a fjord lay before us and soon after we arrived in Kirkenes, under that midnight sun that never stops shining; it was four in the morning and people were out on the streets, sleep was out of the question for us, too, this sun shone through *every* crack. It was impossible to calm my mother, she almost died of joy.

For the entire drive, she'd repeated her siblings' names and wondered who was still alive and who wasn't, a singsong of names and stories, a litany of people from her early years—it was a canon, actually, and I eventually joined in, which wasn't easy because she kept correcting herself, who belonged to whom or didn't, who was born or died when, the living and the dead, a seemingly endless catalogue, a list of all the people she would introduce me to, people we belonged with, from whom we came and to whom we were now returning. A register of ancestors, of people and dates, dates of birth and death and the corresponding stories.

In Fritz's family there were twelve children. In her family, too, there were twelve, *at least* twelve. She now told me all about them and their stories. In 1942, all of these stories had come to their provisional ends, at least her story had ended that year. The stories had continued, but they couldn't be recounted because my mother had been cut off from the continuation of these life stories, except in the case of death notices.

Twelve siblings. The oldest, Aunt Jördis was born in 1898, the youngest in 1922. My mother was born in 1919, she was the second youngest. And when we arrived at four in the morning, one of her brothers, as an opening gambit, asked, *why did you come with the Nazi whore?* They stood in a line, under that midnight sun, he came up to me and as he shook my hand, he whispered into my ear, *get lost with the Nazi whore*. And then Ronnie, her cousin, who was still very young, took me aside and said, *you can stay the night with me*. And we did.

Ronnie, with whom I got along very well, had worked on an oil rig. He was the son of Uncle Fred, who was the reason we'd driven up there. *If you want to see him again, then come quickly.* He'd fled the Nazis, he fled to Russian and had studied in Russia. In the end, he served in the Norwegian parliament. He made it into the Norwegian parliament as a communist. He'd done business with Russia and received the Order of Lenin. The family also had this uncle.

The next day, Uncle Fred's wife—who had invited us—came over and brought us to him. He sat upright in a deep armchair, erect and very marked by his illness. There were stacks of newspapers to the right and left of him. On the table before him was an ashtray holding the Order of Lenin. He received us alertly and said something, a kind of greeting I think, his lips moving slightly and very quickly, he whispered inaudibly at us. Then he didn't open his mouth again. It was an encounter only through our eyes, friendly and intense, a long moment. It was a strain on him, I felt. He clearly felt the need to see my mother again. They sat across from each other for a long time, looking at each other. He was already gone, I felt, wide awake and yet no longer there.

Next was visiting my mother's favourite sister. She had a small, lakeside cabin somewhere, hidden in the forest. I was told how to get there. We drove and found the lake, but there was nothing there, no cabin, no boat, no aunt, only forest. A forest full of mosquitos. And these mosquitoes swarmed around us as if they'd been waiting for us since 1942. We almost killed each other trying to protect one another from these creatures. At some point my mother just couldn't go on. She sat down on a tree stump in the middle of the forest and I continued alone. I knew my aunt had a boat; she went to her cabin by boat every time. After a while, I *found* the cabin as well as the boat and my aunt and I got my mother in the boat.

Then came the reunion. My mother and her favourite sister. They talked for the entire day and the next and the one after. There were no nights. From the next room, it sounded like I was listening to one of her *monologues*. It was impossible to say who was trying to persuade whom of what. It seemed that Aunt Jördis was the only one in this large family who'd stood by my mother over all the years.

I still have a spoon from Aunt Jördis. It's from Kirkenes. There were twelve of them, one for each child. Aunt Jördis gave it to my mother in that forest. It's *the* spoon my mother ate with as a child. And now I feed my animals here with that spoon.

What I realized in that forest: *this* was my mother. That is, she was this *too*; I just hadn't ever experienced her like *this*. She was always a bit alien to me but also not, alien in a new way at least and familiar in a new way. Maybe we were both *different* in that place. In any case, she was a different person, *unconstrained* as I'd never seen her, almost childlike, trusting and simply direct, without the protective layers around her. I saw her *come alive* more and more. Only very early on, right after she'd come back into my life, did I see her *in good moments* as happy and light-hearted as this. Early on, when we were still *just the two of us* in Lustenau, moving from one hole to the next.

Here she saw the part of her family that was well disposed towards her and she would see the others, too, those to whom she'd have to explain herself. All in all, she wanted to *finally arrive*. In any case, for the first time I had the feeling that she *belonged here*. In this forest full of mosquitoes, it was the first time I felt that she belonged anywhere at all. *Here we're at home, we could have been here from the beginning, Heinz*, she said, taking me in her bite-covered arms. It was the first and only time that we hugged each other, my mother and I. Hugging me, she spoke of the *possibilities* there would have been for us in Norway *back then* and between the lines she was no doubt expressing her wish to stay here *now* and start over.

And yet. Here they certainly understood her *language*. But what she had to say—even in Norwegian—they didn't understand or didn't *want* to understand, what she did back then, in getting involved with a German and on top of that *pledged herself* to him, maybe that's what they couldn't forgive her for, that she had *pledged herself* to that Halbsleben after lightning struck and she got pregnant and had to *leave*. They turned a deaf ear to her in Norwegian too, at least that's how it seemed to me, I could only guess at what was said. And she was no different, she turned a deaf ear and looked away, she was good at that, otherwise she wouldn't have survived, not up there and not down in Lustenau. But gradually she did notice that many things weren't as she wished.

She stayed with her sister in the forest a few days more. I was with my cousin, Ronnie, and he explained things to me.

Not only had my mother gotten involved with a German, but her father had also dealt with Germans. He was the mayor. From comrades who were stationed there with my father—there were a few soldiers from Hohenems and Lustenau with him in Kirkenes—I later heard again and again, yes, we knew your grandfather, the mayor, we knew him very well, they always said. And I heard this from Ronnie, too, at the time. They were always in his house. The Nazis invited themselves to the Hörvold family's house, he said. Please, Heinz, leave. Leave with her as quickly as you can. I started the car and we were gone.

The trip back was awful. She came to again only in Saarbrücken, during the play *The Distant Land* by Arthur Schnitzler. The director knew my story. I'd told him about my mother, about the trip and he said to me, *when you get back, take her to the theatre*. I did and she stayed with me a long time in Saarbrücken. In each run, we had two *film stars* on stage, and one was Joachim Hansen from *The Distant Land*. *Hofreiter* was the name of the character he played. He liked me and I idolized him. My mother met him and simply melted. She knew his movies, *Via Mala*, *Stalingrad: Dogs do You Want to Live Forever*, *The Bridge at Remagen* or *Operation Valkyrie*, in which he played the would-be Hitler assassin Count von Stauffenberg.

And then we had open-air performances in the Saarbrücken castle gardens. Claus Wilcke joined us. He was a cult figure at the time because of the television series *Percy Stuart*, he was also the German voice of Elvis Presley, Omar Sharif and Richard Burton and my mother was as infatuated with him as she'd previously only been with Charlton Heston.

In *The Distant Land*, there's a mountain guide who takes a group of tourists into the mountains and a shower of stones fall on them. It's a small role. The scene is set in South Tyrol but we thought I could play it in Lustenau dialect, like this: *Jo, und dänn sind mar uffe. Oan heat's erschlaga. Mi hätt's ou bald erschlaga, und do sind mir in a Stürmi ko. Han i gset, jetz muoß ma renna, sus sind mir alle hia*. That was the *entire* role. In the first rehearsal, Joachim Hansen split his sides laughing, *I don't understand a single word, but it's funny*. My mother was disappointed that I had such a small role. But there were other plays that season in which she saw me play bigger roles. In Gorki's *The Lower Depths* I was *Satine*, or when Claus Wilcke played *Don Juan*, there's a boy, a farm boy who's always a little in the way and also after the women. At some point this *Don Juan* grabs me and beats me, he throws me against a stone wall, again and again he throws me against the wall. And *that* made an impression on my mother, *that I withstood it*. For me, it wasn't a big deal to be thrown against a wall the way I used to throw kittens at walls when I was a child.

That was our good time in Saarbrücken. After a while, she wanted to go home and I couldn't go with her.

The route to visit her in the asylum was familiar to me from my route to the theatre, the *Valduna* was on the way. It began back then and it remained that way, independent of the place and the places where I was living and acting, a detour to the asylum was always on the way. The *destination* was the *Studio Theatre Feldkirch*. Lustenau, Götzis, Klaus, Weiler, Röthis, Sulz. Rankweil. And *after* Rankweil, *back behind Rankweil*, then *not* the fork that leads up to *Valduna*, but straight on ahead to Feldkirch. The plays, the acting and especially the director were my *salvation*. Eugen Andergassen was a famous poet then. We were introduced by Walter Fenz, *the submariner*, the *eternal warrior*, my friend from the embroidery factory, he knew what I longed for, he knew the poet and wrote him. Then I received a letter, I'd be most welcome, the poet would be happy to receive Heinz from Lustenau.

I always spoke *pompelusisch* with Walter. He always said, *adiehala hadierscht*, but never told me what it means. That's how he greeted me and that's how we said goodbye. This saying opened the door to Andergassen for me. But he didn't teach me how to speak *pompelusisch*, he taught me how to speak period, he brought me to language. With my dialect, my 'Lustenauerish,' even people in the next village couldn't understand me back then, but now they could understand what I was saying.

Then came the rehearsals. My boss in the embroidery factory, Oskar, he helped with this, too. I had to stand at the machine. *That* was my place, my task, and after a double shift, I didn't have much left to give. When you need to rehearse, turn off the machine and go, Oskar said, you can make up the work later.

Would Princess Roseblossom deign to take a deep breath? My *first* performance in a *real* play. Until then I'd only done my own little things in the cellar of the chaplain who gave me his accordion.

Three Bags of Lies was the title of the play and it told the story of a recovery. I played a court physician. *Would Princess Roseblossom deign to take a deep breath?* Princess Roseblossom is gravely ill, she suffers from *boredom*, a disease that occurs only in the *uppermost circles*, which I suspect as a court physician although *I* knew better from my own experience since my mother also had this illness. She'd always suffered from a kind of *ennui*, from homesickness, from *longing* for something that wasn't available, not for her. Not wanting to be *here* and *not* being able to go elsewhere, I inherited that from her, too.

As court physician, I always had a stethoscope with me, which I could use on the ailing princess. We made the props ourselves. I wasn't up to it, so Walter made this stethoscope for me out of the silver paper that was also used to make Christmas tree ornaments at the time. It was very sturdy and at least a half meter long and most important, you could hear very well with it. I took it home after every performance. Props belong in the theatre, but I wanted to have the stethoscope on me at all times, I took it everywhere and I auscultated everyone who didn't refuse to let me. *Would Princess Roseblossom deign to take a deep breath?*

I couldn't help the princess with my medical arts, just as no doctors could help my mother, her fits returned, and those fits, they didn't stop. The doctors tried, but the electroshocks didn't help. I learnt this only later, from a patient named Hermann from Lustenau, and he said, Heinz, the shocks didn't help your mother, and they helped me even less.

But the one who could help the princess was Hans, a swineherd who healed her with his *prince apples*. I always searched for these *magical apples* to rid my mother of her *homesickness*. But they didn't exist outside of the play.

In Lustenau there was a dental technician, a dentist actually, who'd been in Norway with Halbsleben and *he*, too, played a role in my fate. Back then, we didn't go to the dentist as often, but I did see him a few times. I had to go for a root canal and it was a root canal in every sense.

Every time he hung the X-ray image that he'd taken of my teeth against the lighted screen next to him, he would point at it with a scaler or a spatula as if a memory had just come back to him because he'd smile briefly then look up and past me as if he wanted to tell me something, but he never did. Then he'd shake his head slightly, always the same, his mouth would become severe and my chair would tilt back and down. And each time he seemed to be drilling down into a kind of trance, as if he were drilling and poking into a memory that my teeth were showing him. He drilled all the way down and through to my Norwegian roots, which he exposed and resealed.

Then he would pull back and raise my chair upright again, now affectionate and gently, always the same, and after examining the results of his efforts, he would say over my head, *he should be ashamed*. That's what he would say without explaining who should be ashamed of what. I didn't have the courage to ask. *He should be ashamed*. With that, he'd send me on my way every time, and later in my thoughts as well, for a while, I'd think of it with every bite.

On a small table in his waiting room there was *one* magazine, not a stack of them, only a single one. The women's magazine *Für Sie*. I'd leaf through it when I had to wait and once I happened on an advertisement. *Wiesbaden Conservatory and Drama School*. My fingers trembling, I tore it out of the magazine and carried it around for a long time before placing it on the embroidery machine that Walter was working on and I had to oil. I had to walk up and down the *oil ditch* in front of the machine with an oil can to keep the machine running, and I set the scrap of paper down in front of him, as if casually, because he had no idea how big a deal it was for me either. The next time I passed him with my oil can, he was already hooked. *Then we'll write to them*. The most important letters in my life were written by others. One day later, the letter was on its way—a few days later the reply came: I should come to Wiesbaden.

The train left from Bregenz. Walter had driven me there. My girlfriend, Christl Singer was already gone; she didn't want to come to Wiesbaden with me and she didn't care for acting. But my mother was happy. Please, go, go, go, she said, *I* always wanted to be an actress and now *you* will be.

Walter had driven me to the station in his white VW, he had a snow white VW, and he wore very special gloves, kid leather gloves, the kind race car drivers wore in those days. He never let me down, not for a second. And I was the one who was leaving.

I knocked on the door in Wiesbaden, it was near the National Theatre on the city park. A friendly man opened the door. Yes, he said and asked what I wanted.

I immediately forgot the little bit of German I'd learnt with Andergassen. The man didn't understand a single word of what I was trying to say to him, he took fright and told me to come back the next day.

It was evening and I was sitting on a bench. I sat on that bench with my suitcase, the suitcase I'd taken from my mother. She'd moved in with this suitcase when she came down from Norway at the time and I was moving out with it now.

A woman came up to me and asked me how I was doing. *Everything's fine, it's fine.*

Come, please, come with me, she said. And she walked, she rushed through the city with me, almost at a run, and I ran with her. After an hour or even longer, we stopped at a door. She rang. A slender man opened the door and went completely pale when he saw me. Come with me, he said and led me through the house, opened a door, then another, and finally we stood in an enchanted little room. I stayed there for three and a half years. I lived with the man and the years with him were the most wonderful time.

It wasn't long before he showed me photographs of his son who'd died in the war and I saw that the boy could have been my brother. The woman recognized this when she saw me on the park bench. She worked for him in his house. A few months earlier, he'd lost his wife. He told me his story and I told him mine, he knew my tale and I knew his. He knew what *Lebensborn* meant, he knew all about it and he knew about my half-siblings. To him I was like a son who has been resurrected, and he was *the* father I'd always wished for.

Very soon I also had a job as a nurse in the municipal hospital. As a nurse's aide. I learnt my first *foreign word* there from another nurse. This nurse was a *giant*, and this giant was also at the drama school. His name was Fleischmann. He always played the great men in the classics, *Herod* and *Caesar*. But he left the school suddenly. Come with me, he said, I'm going to America, America needs young men. I can't go, I told him, I have family at home, I can't leave them. Otherwise, I might have gone with him. I never heard from him again, but sometimes I thought he might be that villain *Jaws* in the James Bond movie. There's always a sinister character and in that one it was *Jaws* who could bite through anything, even steel. And this Fleischmann—he wasn't *Jaws*, but he could have been.

One day, in rehearsal, right in the middle of the play, in the middle of a dialogue with him, he broke off and said, I can't play this scene with you, I just can't say this sentence to you when you're right in front of me like you are now. *Why can't you?* Because I'm addressing you as if you're *the bloom of health*, but you're certainly not the bloom of health. You should be put on display; first stuffed and then displayed, you look so *necrophilic. Necrophilic*. I didn't know what to do with this. The next day, I went to a bookshop and bought a dictionary of foreign words, a very small one, the smallest they had and from then on, I always had it with me. And it told me what I was. My first foreign word told me something about myself or perhaps it *meant* me in general. *Necrophilic. Drawn to death. Death-loving.* And it was true, Fleischmann was right; he truly saw and recognized me for what I was.

On the side he worked as an orderly for the municipal hospital. Maybe you could get me a job there, I asked him one day, I need to earn money.

We can try, but with the risk that they'll admit you right away, as a patient, he said. He brought me with him and I was lucky. The man he introduced me to gave me a job. This man also arranged it so that I could work at all the stations, but most of the time I was in the *psychiatric ward*. It didn't help me get to grips with my psyche, but I did see how many poor devils there were. There was one who constantly repeated: *Come on board for Berlin, come on board for Berlin*, pacing back and forth all the while, up and down, from one room to the next, opening the door, shutting the door, *come on board for Berlin, come on board for Berlin*. And another who always said, *I'm afraid of you, you're Richard III*. I knew I was *necrophilic*. But who was Richard III?

I worked in the psychiatric ward for three years. From seven in the morning until two in the afternoon. In this way, I always felt near my mother because even though I couldn't be with her in Lustenau, I still visited her every day. Whenever I opened the door to a room to find a woman looking at me, it seemed as if she was the one who'd been waiting for me, waiting to *board* and travel together to *Berlin* or to be freed with me from the fear of *Richard III*.

Valduna opened up the door and I came, although not *back for more* and I didn't lie down *in the first free bed*, but I was there from seven in the morning to two in the afternoon, every day, then from three in the afternoon until nine at night I was in the drama school. There, too, I felt as if I were going *to her*, to be on stage with a *giant* and a few *necrophilic* dwarves like me.

The first role that I rehearsed with others was *Valentin* in *Faust*; Gretchen's brother was my first role. My sister is pregnant and has lost her honour. I won't stand for this and I take the *eminent doctor* to task, and with that it was over for me because *Mephisto* guided his hand and his sword. With my last breath, I reproach my sister, blaming her for my death.

In my head, the scene plays out in Kirkenes and Hohenems and in the *Desser colony* in Lustenau on Holzmühlestraße and the best thing would have been if my mother played opposite me. *You're a whore*, Valentin tells his sister to her face. The Heinz in me thought of another *whore* and was grateful to her after all for not drowning him right after he was born as *Gretchen* did to her child in complete despair.

You started secretly with one, soon more will come to join the fun. There was the *secret* Halbsleben, with whom it all started in Kirkenes back then. And there was the secret, the *dissimulated* Russian who drowned somewhere. Then came Fritz. And *after* Fritz, after Fritz was gone, then the rumours started in earnest in the *Desser colony* in Lustenau, *and once a dozen lays you down, you might as well invite the town.*[1]

The next role they rehearsed with me was in *Woyzeck*. There's a journeyman, there are two journeymen in *Woyzeck*, I played the *first*. *The shirt on me back: it isn't mine, and me soul fair stinks of brandy and wine.* That's how he starts in and where it leads—*let us piss on the cross*—he preaches drunkenly at those around him. *In conclusion, dear brethren, let us piss on the cross that a Jew might die.*[2] I played this character, I *embodied* this person from the first sentence to the last. In my *earlier* life. In this journeyman I found myself again, and I auditioned with him again for my *qualifying exams*, which were required at some point. Four or five people in black, men, women, sat in the darkness on their chairs and I auditioned with *Valentin* and the *journeyman*, whose soul stank of more than brandy and wine.

---

1 Johann Wolfgang von Goethe, *Faust* (Walter Kaufmann trans.) (New York: Anchor, 1990).

2 Georg Büchner, *Complete Plays, Lenz and Other Writings* (John Reddick trans.) (London: Penguin Books, 1993).

The final exam was an *improvisation*, that was what they wanted in those days, and I pulled one out of myself, out of what I went through in Lustenau. I told them that my mother had also wanted to be an actress, that she read Åse to me from *Peer Gynt*—Peer Gynt's mother as she *ascends to heaven*—and while I was telling them about her, I became my mother, playing Åse for me. I also became Åse and Peer Gynt, in that scene, she speaks to him, and I was him, too, Åse and Peer Gynt, my mother and me. This scene, in which she says goodbye to him and tries to give him something on the way. In the end, he sits before her lifeless body like an animal that has lost its master.

I played her death as a fit. After all, a fit was my first theatrical experience. When I think of it, I can still see her, the way she—I was four and she had just shown up in my life again—I can see her, the way she came to me in the *Post*, in the small apartment on the top floor, in the garret, where we were accommodated for a time, the way she came *flying down* the steep spiral staircase, weightless, invulnerable, her flight seemed endless, her arms flapped over the banister towards me and above and past me, even after she'd landed, they'd kept flapping for a while. When she opened her eyes, she smiled and tried to explain away what had just happened as a joke or a stunt. *I played that really well.* Dismissing her own illness as a game, performing it or acting as if she were, making a game of what was playing with her, she knew how to do that, and when she saw that I was trying to imitate her *art of flying* and throwing myself down the stairs, we moved into our next accommodations. Even on the ground floor, we couldn't be sure of our safety. We didn't give up our attempts at flight our entire lives long.

My first *role* was performing an epileptic fit. When she was on the ground yet again, contorting herself and twitching before just lying there without moving, I stretched out next to her and moved the way I'd seen her move, then I became still and *my spirit fled*, I lay motionless next to her, waiting to see if she would get up again. And when she did sit upright and smoothen her dress, joking about the way she'd fallen or lain there, she would say, I pulled that off well. She said it each and every time.

It was often impossible to say if she'd actually only been *acting*. And when I imitated her and lay there and she couldn't tell if I'd *play-acted well* or *really had fallen* out of some necessity, not for fun, when I took it too far and acted there and then as if I wouldn't *come to again*, she would say that it was good, that I'd *played* it well and had *won*. If I kept at it, relishing the fear I'd sparked in her, she'd start tickling my entire body in order to force me back to life and freeing us both in fits of laughter. After, we'd lie there, we'd lie next to each other for a long time, exhausted but alive, breathing and listening to each other breathe, and it was good.

I wasn't doing anything *here* other than portraying Åse's death of as one of my mother's fits. Then I stood up and laughed the way she'd always laughed. Then I gestured towards the invisible rising mother and said, *and here: Gerd Hörvold Fritz*. That's exactly how I said it. *Gerd Hörvold Fritz*. The men and women were still sitting in the darkness below and one of them said, yes, it makes sense for you to become an actor.

There and then I wrote my mother a long letter. And she wrote back. It was my only letter from her; I don't think I received a second one. It was partly in Norwegian, partly in the way she was able to think and write and draw in order to communicate how happy she was that I'd made it. She had season tickets for the cinema, and I'd now be in the theatre all season long. It was a little as if I'd crept out of the cage *for her* and the small door was still open for one of us and therefore for both of us.

We both became more alive. It was a time when we didn't become *sicker*. And yet, when I left Lustenau, I had told her I'd come back to her and my siblings and that's how that happened. *She* was the reason, there was no other, not in all the years after. She had sent me away herself; *I* was gone, but *she* was still trapped. I shouldn't have—she'd *always* needed me—I *never* should have gone to drama school, I shouldn't have left her, I felt this all the more clearly at that point. But that didn't help her at all.

In conclusion, dear brethren, let us piss on the cross that a Jew might die. Through this journeyman, things surfaced again, my stepfather's sentences were in my head again like a foul odour that had once been *my* odour. And with *this very* sentence, I did my *qualifying exam.*

But it also revived the memory of a film. *Judgment at Nuremberg.* The way those men, practically the walking dead, come out of the barracks, the crematoria, the piles of shoes and eyeglasses, the crates of dental gold, and that giant excavator, a bulldozer pushing a sheer mountain of naked corpses over a square and into a ditch—images taken by the Allies after the camps were liberated. *You know, Heinz, way too few Jews were gassed.* I was twelve the first time I heard this. It was in my head and even on my tongue at twelve and thirteen, at fourteen, even later. I heard it day and night in those days. And now, at nineteen, in this film I saw and *understood* what had actually happened. At least I had a *sense* of it now.

Prosecution calls the witness, Rudolph Petersen. With this sentence, the witness enters the courtroom. The subject is his forced *sterilization. Prosecution calls the witness, Rudolph Petersen.* I saw the film so many time that this sentence is *my* shorthand for confronting my mother's story.

Montgomery Clift plays the man who has been castrated. With the shorthand sentence, he enters the courtroom as witness for the prosecution. He is clearly very unsure. He takes the stand and is put under oath. His father was a Communist, he says and after some prompting, he adds that in 1933 right *before* the Nazis came to power, he got in a fight with some SA men who'd broken into his parents' apartment to take his father away. He and his brother, however, were able to chase off the thugs. Soon after, once the Nazis were in power, he had to go to an office to apply for a driver's license. One of the officials he meets there is one of the thugs from earlier. This official opens an investigation that ends with the sterilization of the witness. The judge who ordered the *procedure* is present in the courtroom as a defendant.

After the prosecution, the defence counsel questions the witness. With his line of questioning, he tries to make the witness appear *feeble minded* in order to justify the actions of his client who was responsible for the sterilization of the mentally incompetent. The task of the Health Court was to sterilize the mentally incompetent. He asks the witness about his mother, what she died of, whether it was from *natural causes*. The witness says that she died of a weak heart. When the defence counsel claims that she suffered from *hereditary feeble-mindedness*, the witness breaks down because that purported diagnosis served as grounds for his sterilization.

In his distress, the witness takes a photograph from his jacket pocket, a picture of his mother, and shows it to everyone around him, the defence counsel, the accused, and because none of them react, he turns to the judge and demands that he say whether his mother was *feeble minded* or not. *Was she?*

I saw the witness with his mother's photograph and thought of Doctor Gunz who did not take me away back when I lay on the kitchen floor with my mother; he's stable, he stays here, he said. I thought of that when the witness held his mother's picture out to everyone in the room. In the end, he held it out to *me*. It was the photograph of *my* mother that he showed me, the photograph from her suitcase, *our* picture. *I want that you tell me . . . was she feeble minded? . . . Was she?* That's the only question I'd asked myself time and again when she was taken away and brought back changed, because I too, thought that it wasn't only her fits that changed her.

My mother would have been a *candidate* for Doctor Vonbun, who sent them all to Hall and to Hartheim. His mother-in-law was a patient in Valduna and he selected her too, for transport. He diagnosed his own daughter with *heredity mental deficiency* and had her murdered in Munich, and just before the end of the war he tried to have his wife gassed. As an epileptic, my mother would also have been a candidate.

But she was lucky that she was away in the years after my birth, because had things been different, then she would have been *gone*, too, or she would have been *a different person* than the one I knew. She wouldn't have come back into my life, or she would have come back *sterilized* and I wouldn't have had a brother and a sister, my half-siblings wouldn't have existed.

She came to Hohenems in 1942. By then Vonbun had already *cleaned up* both *Valduna* and the general region. In 1941, he had the patients put on *transports*. But he continued taking private trips throughout the surrounding area, word spread, his *visits* to nursing and rest homes were renowned and feared. People often ran away from the homes, fearing they'd be taken away. Maybe word had gotten to my mother and maybe *that* was one reason she disappeared right after I was born.

Here I could see what would have happened to her, what danger she was in, and at the same time, it was an example of what she *took part in*, of what she let herself in for, when she got involved with Halbsleben and *Lebensborn*. After all, she'd been *examined* in Norway when it came to being admitted into *Lebensborn* and she was deemed *racially and ideologically valuable*. Without this valuation, *Lebensborn* would not have supported her.

She did not mention *epilepsy* during this *examination*. The attacks only set in later, after the accident in Berlin on her way south from Oslo, that's where it happened. *Since then, I am the way I am,* she always said, *since then, I can fly, and now that I can fly, my feet no longer touch the ground.*

I watched that film again and again. In every performance of these *court proceedings*, I was present. And I always watched Montgomery Clift, watched how he *became* Rudolph Petersen. His *witness* was so *real*, just as my mother's fits were *real*. Montgomery Clift was my first role model.

I wanted to elicit what this film elicited in me, or at least be able to suggest it and this, I thought, should be possible in a film, in a play.

And then, years later, I acted in such a play. In a small theatre company, which we took on the road a lot. *Do You Know the Milky Way?* By Karl Wittlinger. A *homecoming play,* as they were called then. After more than ten years, a man comes home from the war, he returns to his village, but he is no longer officially recognized there. He no longer exists. He has been declared dead, his possessions dispersed, and he's unwelcome in the village. He poses a challenge to the new order that was established in his absence. He no longer belongs there.

A play for two actors. A doctor. A patient. An asylum.

I was the patient for whom there was no homecoming. I come from another planet. At least that's what I claim. My psychiatrist, the doctor and all the other roles were played by my colleague Michael, who later took his own life. He was also from another planet. He was the only actor I met who had a past like mine. We sensed it in each other without ever talking about it. One night, after the show, he broached the topic with me. In the dressing room. He sat before his mirror and was in the process of slipping out of the role. He spoke to me with the words of *my* returnee, with a sentence that *I* had said to him as my psychiatrist onstage an hour earlier. *Your life story—it gave me the idea. When I read through it, I thought to myself: he's also someone who doesn't belong—just like me.* And as my doctor he adds: *What seems important to me is that such disagreeable cases occur again and again—down below, in the fog: that someone has to go before his time, just because 'the others' don't want him.*

I'm half Norwegian, I said. And I'm half Polish—maybe, he said. In his case it was this: his *mother* was from Berlin. But he didn't know whether or not he had the *right* mother, his own parents. Maybe he was a *stolen* child, taken from a family in Poland or some other occupied territory and brought to Berlin and given to this *mother*, to be *Germanized*, as it was called at the time. Once, during a performance, after the end of a scene behind the curtain, he'd alluded to this. Maybe

I was once *at home* in Poland very early in my life, he'd said. I was dug up there and replanted. Repotted, he said. But the garden I'd been pulled up from, the family there, it was no longer the same soil. He didn't know or wouldn't say more. In any case, he was devoted to the woman from Berlin.

In the play, as this returnee, I take on odd jobs at fairgrounds and amusement parks to make ends meet. As a *death driver*. Back then, there were men—usually two of them—who rode their motorcycles through large tubes or on a wire strung over the spectators' heads. I almost die at one of these *shows* because in a sense I'd been trying to, given that I was never able to get a permanent footing anywhere.

Michael knew the feeling. The scene with the looming accident exhausted him every time. Even though Michael had to play a tough guy, the second *death driver* who can't show any emotion, you could tell that it was hard on him. One day he said that he had to stop for a while. And not very long after that, Michael was gone.

Two other Norwegian women who'd probably gone through something similar to my mother lived in the area, two women that I know of. One in Nenzing. And one in Dornbirn. Neither lived with the biological father of the children for whom they'd come down from Norway. The children were *stepchildren*. They lived with *stepfathers*. But there were also some *stepstories* that worked out.

We often took the train to visit the woman in Nenzing, my mother and I. These trips were always exciting for me. She died young, that Norwegian woman. She came from *southern Norway*. I don't know where the other one came from, but she was likely from the south. Only my mother was from the *north*.

The man in Nenzing was a football player for *FC Nenzing*. The team's still around. The football pitch is also still there. She lived right next to it. She was probably my mother's best friend at the time. Her husband was a good man. They were all still young then. I was a child. And this Norwegian woman, she always did the football players' laundry. In my memory, I only see her as hanging up the washing with my mother helping her. On the wash line behind the house, hung the entire team. Whenever we visited, she'd always just finished *a huge load*. And while the two of them spoke to each other in Norwegian, I would stretch out under the jerseys and shorts that fluttered above me in the wind and I'd shoot or get one goal after another in the game I imagined myself playing, but in reality never did back then.

The woman in Nenzing had a son. I got along well with him. One day he disappeared. He emigrated very early. Like me in Lustenau, he just couldn't stand being in Nenzing any longer. He left when his mother was still alive.

And in Dornbirn, the other Norwegian woman, we didn't go to visit her, she came to us. She had a daughter my age. When was that— I was twelve. By the time I was thirteen, fourteen, they were no longer around. They emigrated to Canada. This means that very soon, my mother was alone in Vorarlberg, *as a Norwegian*, I mean. When my mother died, I wrote them a letter. I still had their address. But I didn't get any more mail from them.

Whether or not this daughter was also a *Lebensborn child*, I can't say. In any case, she was a *stepdaughter*. And her mother, I could have looked at her for hours with her *enormous*, dark eyes. I couldn't get enough of looking at her. And the daughter, she had her mother's eyes.

There was also a Norwegian woman in Hohenems. I only learnt of her when I played *The Milky Way* in Lustenau. There, too, I *came back* as an unwelcome *returnee*; we performed in the town hall.

After the last performance, a man introduced himself as kin, a *kindred spirit*, and said he wanted to tell me something about my mother, whom he'd met as a child, as he put it. He had an early memory of *the Norwegian woman* that he'd like to share with me. So we met the next day in front of this man's sawmill in Hohenems, in the middle of the forest, on the road up to Emsreute. This was all part of my *Transylvanian domain*, my father's domain, I knew this, I felt it too, and was accordingly uneasy.

The man was waiting for me in the forecourt of his sawmill. *Our family mill*, he said even before offering his hand, there was a mill here in 1500 and over time the mill became a mill and a sawmill. Only the stream has remained the same.

From the forecourt I looked up at a solitary structure on a steep forest slope and recalled there had often been a rumour that it might have been a home, a *Lebensborn maternity home*. As if he could read my thoughts he said, no, it wasn't that kind of place. I'm an immediate neighbour, I spent my childhood in the house next door, I'd have noticed something. The building was called *Einfirst*, he said. For a while, sick or disabled children were housed there but that was *after* the war. *During* the war, from '39 on, the *Einfirst* was managed. That lasted until the occupation. It was run as an inn. Renovated. Beautiful views. The claim that it was a home for such children during the war, for the *Lebensborn*, is news to me, he said. Although children from Cologne and Essen were often sent here during the war through the *children evacuation program*. But they were mostly housed in the *Post* or the *Kreuz*.

Our *family seat* in my grandfather's house was a large and open house, the owner of the sawmill said. Because of the construction company he ran, he had an active social life. Even very early on, people came to use the telephone because he had the first, and for a long time, the only telephone in the area. There were also many relatives. You must know, my *grandfather* had three wives, he said. With the first wife he had two children, a son and a daughter. This woman died young, but of what, we don't know. With the second, he had six children. She also died. He married again. With the third wife he had another son. *My* father was the oldest child of the *second* wife, he said. My grandfather was the linchpin of the family. He was its centre. On Sunday afternoons, everyone gathered in his house. My father had a saw, this lumber mill belonged to my father before me, he said. Other relatives had a construction materials business and so they'd all meet to discuss things that they might need to deal with in the coming week. And *your* grandfather was also part of this *circle*, the man said,

Anton Halbsleben senior was also part of it. *My father was the god father of Anton junior, that is of your father*, he said. Halbsleben senior, *your* grandfather, did butchering for locals. It was only seasonal work because the smaller farms did their *home slaughtering* primarily in the fall. The pigs that had been bought as *piglets*, the three or four farrow, were ready for slaughter in the autumn and during the winter, provisions were made for the following year, the bacon and sausages prepared and much else. *Your* grandfather was at the Hohenems-Reute, he was their *house butcher*. In the winter, he stored his machine, the sausage machine he used to make the house sausage, with us. And during the rest of the year, I remember that in spring or over the summer, when there was no demand for butchering, that he also worked as a logger for us. We had our own woodlands, as he called it, *our private woodlands*. Anton senior also worked in the sawmill. He was from Ebnit. The Halbslebens come from Ebnit. Then they moved to Emser Reute and from there down into the valley.

With us, it was *all interwoven*, business and family, and that's why we knew everything about family matters. At Christmas or New Year's, Anton junior stayed with us. It was the custom for children to visit their godparents on New Year's Day to *wish them a happy new year*. The godchildren would be given a new year's gift, usually milk bread, a plaited loaf, and on New Year's Day this braided loaf would be shaped like a wreath. As children we happily hung those wreaths around our necks and wore them home with pride. As we got older, over the years, the gifts of wreaths stopped. But as godchildren, we'd visit our godparents on New Year's Day until we got married and at the wedding, the godparents were expected to give one more gift, in farewell, so to speak. I remember very clearly the godchildren coming to our house one after the other on New Year's morning. Anton came too, in the morning he'd visit my father and congratulate him. It was a constant coming and going. The older ones were offered a small glass of liqueur, the bread was served with a call for *solidarity* in the next year.

And then, during the war, I was still young, born in '32, the sawmill owner said—*when was Norway?*

1940, I told him, I was born in December '42.

So then 1942, he said. Yes, I was ten and I remember that over in the *family seat* they talked about Anton, that he'd found a wife or a girlfriend in Norway. Then we heard *she's coming*. And *expectations* were expressed in the family circle, a *Norwegian*, that was something special—for me as a child anyway it was, he said. And then we heard *she's here*. I remember exactly where I *saw* her for the first time. In the small vestibule, right behind the front door there was a small vestibule with stairs to the upper floor before the parlour. She was there in front me, unexpectedly. The parlour was filled with people waiting for *the Norwegian woman*, and there she was, alone in the vestibule. There was no one with her. She stood before me just like the wall behind her. Tall, imposing, a very beautiful woman in my eyes as a ten-year-old, the man said. It must have been right at the beginning. I remember the parlour was full of people. Back then, as a child you weren't included in the adults' conversations. When the grown-ups spoke, children were supposed to be silent, he said, so on such occasions I would disappear behind a door and listen to the conversations from there, that was my way then and it was *my* spot—between the wall and the door—my hiding place. And when I wanted to get back amid *the action*, I swung the door into the room and, unnoticed, mingled with the others. That's how it was back then too, when I saw the *Norwegian woman* for the first time, he said.

He always referred to the *Norwegian woman*. Even though he knew that he was talking about my mother, he always called her the *Norwegian woman*. I stood in the corridor, leaning against the wall behind the door, listening to the others, he said, thinking I was alone. And when I came out from behind the door, she was standing across from me on the other side of that small corridor, her eyes closed, and when she opened her eyes, she seemed startled, probably because she didn't know how long I'd been watching her. We stood there for quite a while, without a word, and then she smiled, nodded at me and put a finger to her lips. At that moment, the doorbell rang, and the noise and the others' joy released us.

For me, she was an *apparition*, like I'd never seen before, the man said. Even now, I see her standing there. Imposing, tall, a very beautiful woman. And I remember the silver fox fur she wore. Fox fur had just come into fashion. When they went to church, it was winter at the time, women would drape a fox around them. That's why it made such an impression on me, seeing the tall woman with a beautiful fur coat.

Our soldiers, I can call them *our* soldiers, who were stationed in Norway, he said, gave their brides or wives these furs as gifts, a *silver fox* as they were called. *Half of Hohenems* wore a *silver fox* to church on Sundays. And the other half, the men, were up in Norway. The Norwegian woman also wore one of these *silver foxes*.

That was my *first* impression, he said. I later saw her—not very often, but every now and again—I saw her with the family and here in our house and both here and there we were happy to see her. Here she was *welcome*. How she was received by the *Halbsleben* family, I don't know but no doubt *warily*, he said then, looking me straight in the eye. What was her religion?

Protestant, I said. According to her papers, she was Protestant.

That was surely the difficulty, then, *in those days*, he said. But I don't have to tell you that, you grew up here. But then, after your father's separation from the Norwegian woman, our family's relationship with him cooled. She no longer came to my grandfather's house as often and we didn't see her here anymore either. She was *only mentioned again* after Anton came back from the war. I don't know how it all came about, *the separation*, he said, but I *do* know that people looked askance at him because of it. They judged him harshly for it. He *brought her down here*, took her away from her homeland, *for what, actually*, they asked. But then the war was over and with that, things with the Norwegian woman were over too. And she didn't *want* to go back, after the war, he said, maybe it was like the women were brought here as *forced labourers*, the *Eastern European slave labourers* who found *relationships* here, they couldn't return home after the war either because they'd be ostracized there as wives of Germans. Often the mere fact that they'd worked *for the* enemy was enough for them to disappear into a camp or have their children taken away from them.

After the separation, my father's relationship to his godson changed, we all sensed it, he said. The separation and then the *new* relationship, the marriage, had an effect. Only when the *other* woman's children were older, was your father invited back. *The Norwegian woman* disappeared then. She even vanished from our stories. All we knew was that she was somewhere in Lustenau, that was much we knew, and maybe no one wanted to know any more than that.

My father's *mother*, I interjected, *your* father's godson's mother, *she* was the reason that *he* left *the Norwegian woman*. I'm talking about Halbsleben's mother, I said.

About *your* grandmother, yes, I knew her, he said, but I can't speak to her *attitude*, however—it's entirely *possible* that it wasn't easy for her, at the time, I mean. That's why I asked about your mother's *faith* before. Until the Second World War, that is, until that time, *Protestants* were despised almost as much as *Jews*. There was the saying: *Utter fressen d' Luther—Prodders eat udders*. A cow's udder is the last thing anyone would want at table. The saying surfaced again around the end of the war when meat rations kept getting smaller. Then even *udders* were offered. Smoked. That's when the saying gained currency again. *Utter fressen d' Luther*.

So the Norwegian woman was a *Lutheran*, he said, looking up at a small cluster of houses in the forest above us. The people who lived on those plots up there on the slope, he said, it's not far from here to there, but they were *separate*. In their belief, too. They were much more *Catholic* than people down here in the valley. *Hatred of the Jews* was deeply ingrained there, the Church's anti-Semitism, and Anton's mother was surely imbued with it, he said, I believe she came from a devout Catholic family. These matters of religion, it was actually *inconceivable*, that someone would bring a Lutheran into the family. It was like the organization *Die Flamme*, which still exists, and the Catholics that joined *Die Flamme*, they were known in the community and ostracized accordingly. Until 1929 those who wanted to be cremated were excommunicated.

Then again, these women who came back with our soldiers from Norway or from Germany and from other countries also brought new blood after the workers who'd come up from Trentino with their wives around 1900. A few of the women brought here as *forced labourers* stayed here after the war. And there were a great many of them, he said and gestured towards the old mill next to the saw. Right up there, in the factory building, Belgian prisoners of war were imprisoned from the first years of the war, then French, Serbian and Russian, one after the other. And *then* the *forced labourers* were here, Ukrainian slave labourers. The men and the women were used for agricultural work, placed in the nursing home and on farms. Up here they were put to work for the *Otten* company, he said, manufacturing the so-called *Volksgasmaske*. Each resident was to be provided with a *people's gas mask* for the *final battle*. These *masks* were manufactured up there, out of rubberized fabric, the masks were die cut there and then the *eyes* were inserted like *spectacles*. The *filter*, the crucial part, was attached later. Here, just the *masks* were produced. They came in small wooden crates with a lid and instructions for use. All produced here, in the *lower* factory, he said. The *people's gas masks* were made by the forced labourers. Some toiled up there in the factory, the others were put to work in the community's poor house or agricultural operations. In the morning, they were collected by tractor from the *Rheinhof* and driven back in the evening. They had beautiful voices, the owner of the sawmill said, they sang their Ukrainian songs in the cart. They weren't bullied, not up there, there was no word of that. As children we knew that Ukrainians always had sunflower seeds in their trouser pockets, he said, apparently, they were given enough sunflower seeds because now and then they'd slip us a few. And they had their own tobacco, *Machorka*, terrible stuff.

A master baker lived in the village. He was a Nazi sympathizer, and he delivered the bread for the forced labourers. This baker—I heard this from the man who carried the bread up there as a boy—he said, this baker always put in a few extra rolls for the labourers so that they wouldn't run short. He risked imprisonment because the rules governing the way you were supposed to treat these poor people were very strict. Merely *speaking* with them was often grounds for prosecution. *Don't look them in the eye*, we were constantly told, *do not meet their eyes*. Of course we looked these people straight in the eye.

But not everyone was like the master baker, he said, there was an owner of a large farm who engaged many of these forced labourers, he gave them very little and exploited them. They called him the *Russian Farmer*.

At the end of the war, his house burned down.

The women, the Ukrainian women, who could go back after the war or rather who *had to return*, some of them left their children here out of fear that they'd be taken away at home. A few of these *Eastern labourers* remained after the war, he said, for some it was better here than it would have been in Ukraine. They'd *worked for the enemy*.

Do you know of other women who came down from Norway *because of a relationship*, I asked the sawmill owner. I think my mother was the only one who came to Hohenems from Norway. Or do you know of others?

Gader, he said. *Gader*. He also brought a Norwegian woman down here. That woman also came from Norway. And stayed here. Johansson.

Also a *silver fox*? I asked. Yes, also a *silver fox*.

Following my conversation with the sawmill owner, I went looking for the house of the Norwegian woman he mentioned. I passed the butcher shop that I'd passed on my search for my *father* and remembered how he wordlessly *flew through me* with his sides of pork wings. So once again, I stood in front of this building, which had both attracted and repelled me over the years after I'd met him in it. I briefly considered going in again and trying one more time with him and with us, if only to leave once again with a few sausages and a pickle as I had the first time. But I continued on to the Norwegian woman's house. She lived just a few steps from away from Halbsleben,

I realized. She was surely *welcome*, I thought, and I also thought of the *udder-eating Lutherans* and of how often this same story must have played out around us.

If there was more to be learnt, then it would be from people like this sawmill owner who were there but not *fully there*, not in the innermost circle, and for that reason, may have been willing to speak more freely. That's also what my half-sister, Ingrid from Hohenems, suggested when I told her what I'd learnt about my mother from this *kindred spirit* and about the role *her* father's mother, *our* grandmother, may have played.

Ingrid told me no more than I already knew. My grandma hated your mother, she said, she wanted to be rid of both of you and that's why you both disappeared. We learnt this *only recently* from the neighbours, she said, thirdhand so to speak. It was difficult with my father. The answers, I knew, would not come. But I had an aunt, my godmother, and I asked her, starting even as a child and through the years, repeatedly, and then, after I'd met you, I tried again but it didn't come from her. I put a lot of *effort* into getting an answer and would rather have learnt it from within the family, but things like this always come from outside. Sometimes I think that *others* know more than those who were directly involved.

It all relates to the very beginning in Hohenems. I was born in Hohenems, apparently. This too I learnt *only recently* from local people and I was disappointed that no one was willing to open their mouths, then or since, until now, especially your father's sister, your aunt, who would also have been *my* aunt. She must have known a lot, she said, this aunt lived in Hohenems, was married and had three children of her own. I had a good relationship with her, she was always ready to help and I liked her very much.

My father simply brought her along, this woman, *your* mother. He always told us that he wanted to save her, that otherwise she'd have been—*lost*. In any case, it wouldn't have worked out well for her. Of course, it didn't work out well for her anyway.

I never knew my grandparents, she said, but still, I have an *idea* of them, of how they might have been and I don't see them in that kind of light. According to what I was told, my grandmother was always a victim. She nearly died because my father was in the war. Her only son. She suffered a great deal, I think, and died soon after the war. But whether she did *that*—I'm a mother of two sons and can't imagine that anyone would treat a daughter-in-law that way, one who is very poor, after all, because she comes from far away and doesn't understand the language and is actually at their mercy. I can't understand it, she said, but I'd have liked to hear it from my own relatives. In fact, I believe that almost everyone in Hohenems knew. I heard plenty of allusions. It's just odd that of the *ones* who were alive at the time and who lived through it, very few said anything. And those who are speaking *now* are their children; they heard it from their parents and are now telling us about it.

But *then*, Ingrid said, before we saw each other for the first time, before we first met, just before then, a woman spoke to me, a woman from Hohenems. She said she was very sorry but she had to deliver a difficult message. She said that I probably didn't know that I had another brother in Innsbruck. She approached me so *carefully*, Ingrid said, that I found it funny, since I'd known all along. It wasn't news to me. We'd always known. At home, it wasn't a secret, but the facts weren't *mentioned*.

A few days *before* our first meeting, my half-sister Ingrid got in touch with me and said that *her father would like to meet me*. I was sixty, I'd just moved from Münster to Innsbruck and there I'd met Rudolf Radtke, the usher in the theatre, who's from Hohenems and who told me that I wasn't Halbsleben's but the *son of a Russian who drowned*. His wife or whoever had probably mentioned me to Ingrid because he said that he knew her and would speak to her.

After that, Ingrid got in touch with me. Until then I'd had no contact with my father, not for sixty years. For this first encounter, this first meeting, I sent Ingrid the photograph of my mother and me. She then showed it to her mother. Her mother was already ill, she said, she was bedridden and we nursed her, then I showed her the photograph. Father was there too. And she had a good laugh. She was very ill and rarely laughed anymore. But then she had to laugh. My father and you, you had the *same* face. My mother saw this. And she laughed, she couldn't stop, she seemed freed. I believe that meant that he couldn't deny it. He had to admit it. My father met my mother *after* the war. And for both of them, it was their great love. He cared for her and looked after her until her death. She was ten years younger than he was. A great love story, that's how we experienced it as children. My mother was a very open-minded woman, she said. My mother would have been the last one not to have taken you in. If she'd known how it was for you in Lustenau. But you see, when you don't communicate, there's no way to change anything. When you don't *know*. Or don't *want* to know. In my parents' case, it has to be said, maybe they didn't *want* to know. My parents remained silent, and we didn't want to hurt them with questions. But back then, as a *child*, she said, it would never have *occurred* to me that you might not be doing well. I knew that you existed. I assumed that you had as good a family as I did, I couldn't imagine any other possibility. For us, you simply weren't present. You were alive. You existed. But not in our world.

Where the two of you had gone, where you'd ended up, how much *my* aunt might have known, is something I'd also like to know. In any case, you weren't with *her*. That would have been talked about. She had three young children and a husband. He was a person of that time. I can't imagine that he'd have been willing. But *then* you two moved into a neighbour's house, she said, three or four doors down from where our grandmother lived. You were in the house of a woman named Mina. I knew her. She had a brother. Both were single, never married. Mina took in the Norwegian woman and her child, that's what the neighbours say and I have to believe them because they say it independently of each other.

How *long* both of you stayed with Mina and her brother must not have been very long because they were very poor, they really had nothing at all. Our father helped them repeatedly.

I no longer live in the area, Ingrid said, but my sister still lives there. She asked around and the neighbours said that they don't know what happened *afterward*, after you left Mina's, *none* of them know, not even those who are talking now.

How did you find me, I asked the man from Hohenems, who showed up on my doorstep one afternoon and wanted to find out something about my mother's journey down from Norway and about *Lebensborn* in general.

I work in the city archives, the man said, and in the archives *a historian from Hohenems* told me that *his brother* lived in Innsbruck and at a theatre performance there he met a man who ostensibly is a *Lebensborn child* and looking for the home where he would have been. We said that we, in the archives, don't know of any such a home. But the thought stuck with me, so I started looking and set out on my search. And there he was, standing before me.

This archivist, he might be *the third hand* that Ingrid spoke about, this external source of help with things that have been kept secret, I thought and so we agreed to meet in Hohenems. However, I asked that it be on *neutral ground*, and if there is none, then at least not on that spot.

He was waiting for me in a café on Bahnhofstraße and when I entered, I remembered passing the café with my friend Franz Jäger on his moped, looking for my father. We'd ridden to the train station back then. There we turned back, I'd imagined picking my mother up from the train and continuing the journey to my father's butcher shop with her. In that fashion, she was with me this time too.

On the table before him lay her *itinerary* from Oslo to Hohenems, which I'd given him at our first meeting.

I'm very happy to have this document, the man said, it's the first indication of a *Lebensborn* case here in Hohenems or even Vorarlberg. Maybe it's mentioned elsewhere but in there are no traces in the files. The writing had to be made visible again. The letter is so worn and tattered that it's barely legible. Someone must have carried it with them for a very long time. I also find it interesting because we have another document in a similar condition in the archives, he said, almost transparent, it belonged to a man from Hohenems who was executed in 1944 because he listened to a Churchill speech on *Swiss Radio*. He wrote, today at five o'clock in the evening, I will be killed and now some person from Hohenems will be happy because he was always following me and finally denounced me. That's also a letter from that time, the archivist said, he'd written to a friend from Dornbirn and this friend carried the letter around in his jacket pocket for twenty years. This itinerary fascinates me because it offers detailed guidance for the trip and for the way these people think, for the system's processes, he said. In the meantime, I've searched for other sources in Hohenems and the woman in the parish archives, in the rectorate, was a stickler for privacy protection. I asked for permission to see the entry for 9 December 1942 in the baptismal registry. She would have to cover something, she said, it contained something that could *not* be seen. It's the only piece of your mother's information that I don't have, but all the rest is here, the archivist said. It's all verified. Beyond this, there are no records of her in the parish.

But as to the child's *father*—he recognized the child—there is no doubt; the report, military postcode, it's all available. It's interesting that his denial came later. The story about the Russian who drowned.

The documents were before him on the table. There were also photographs and copies of old engravings of the *Valduna*, I noticed.

We can't help you in your search for the home because there was *likely* no such home in all of Vorarlberg. But *Lebensborn*—that's unequivocal, he said, tapping the travel plan with both hands. *The Higher SS and Police Leader in the Reich Commissariat for the Occupied Norwegian Territories, Lebensborn Division*—that's completely clear, he said. I was just surprised that they also supported people who weren't in the *SS* but were *simple* Wehrmacht soldiers. *You* may have thought your father was in the *SS*, for which the program had initially been intended but they implemented it for all the soldiers since they *wanted* the Norwegian women to come south, provided they met the program's *criteria*. It's important to me to have these documents in hand, he said. How meticulously it was all planned and carried out, the connections, the train departures, and the directives to all the different places where the woman should be assisted on her way. Your mother would *not* have been treated very well up there.

I know, I said. My father brought her down out of *pity*, as people are always trying to convince me here.

He'd have thought that they'd welcome her here, the archivist said. He would not have expected his own mother's rejection. It appears that his mother, that *your* grandmother was against it. She objected to a marriage. But the *thoroughness* with which it was all organized, this meticulousness, made an impression on me, he said. The list of connections alone. According to this document, your mother started her journey on 5 October 1942. Her journey lasted until 8 October and on *9 December* you were born in Hohenems. That wasn't much time, he said and kept reading the itinerary. *Miss Gerd Hörvold is travelling from Oslo to Hohenems. The timetable is as follows:*

5.10.42 Oslo East Station dep. 16.10. Sleeping car. Ferry. Train change. Overnight stay, train change, train change, overnight stay. *Lindau dep. 13.14, Hohenems arr. 14.21*, he said, speaking more to himself and as if in confirmation, he softly read each word. *I request that the offices of the NSV and the Red Cross assist Miss Hörvold in transferring from the boat to the train, exchanging currencies and obtaining food ration cards.*

I request that the District Command in Copenhagen find Miss Hörvold overnight accommodations should she miss the connecting train at 11.00.

The Munich office of the NSV is requested to find overnight accommodations. A telegram will be sent separately.

The Hohenems office is requested—should Miss Hörvold not meet her fiancé, Private Anton Halbsleben, in Berlin—to take charge of her until she is collected by her in-laws, the Anton Halbsleben family, Defreggerstraße 28, who have been informed of her arrival by telegram.

Defreggerstraße 28. She must have lived there at least until she gave birth, the archivist said. She probably went to the hospital from there and left soon after.

I request that all offices of the Wehrmacht, the Party, the NSV and the Red Cross stand by Miss Hörvold in word and deed until she reaches her destination.

How prudently it's all thought through, he said, and what a friendly, almost affectionate, tone they use—*I request, is requested, I request*—the friendly tone these people used with each other never fails to irritate me, all the same, this is an SS document.

The office of the NSV in Hohenems mentioned here, I asked, where was it and most importantly, who exactly was being addressed with these words?

The Hohenems office is requested—should Miss Hörvold not meet her fiancé, Private Anton Halbsleben, in Berlin—to take charge of her. NSV. National Socialist People's Welfare. At the time, this was the mayor himself, the archivist replied after considering it for a long time, the mayor was the *Ortsgruppenleiter*, the local group leader of the NSV.

And if it's all a mistake, I ask, and my mother never arrived, not to that street and not to that address?

These are *your mother's* particulars, the archivist said. When giving birth, one is *required* to give an address. This address is noted in her files and we can go there. And here on the itinerary, this address and the same names are given. And *then* she would have left. *After* your birth.

Defreggerstraße 28. We now stood in front of the house. A quiet, tidy neighbourhood and I had no doubt whatsoever that this was my first time here. In any case, that's how it felt. We could hear the laughter of children playing in the surrounding gardens. A woman came out of the house and, without paying us any attention, passed in the direction we had come from.

Other people live here now who have nothing to do with this story, the archivist said.

I also noticed where the laughter was coming from. In the neighbouring garden, two young children ran across a daisy-covered lawn to a swing in the middle of the yard that swung back and forth above the grass. The children's heads were barely higher than the grass.

We stood before the lovingly renovated, shingle-clad house. My mother must have entered through this gate. She could have sat on the bench next to it in her silver fox fur. I tried to remember. I couldn't. My half-sister was right: you *can't* remember this time because you would have been less than a year old, she would say when we talked about the early years in Hohenems. She couldn't understand the suspicions and fantasies that I associated with those years or why I had images and memories like the sense of being *rocked* by a woman who was both unfamiliar and familiar. You *can't* have memories of it, Ingrid would say each time. And yet that's how it was and how could it be any different, I *experienced* it. I remembered being rocked by a woman who wasn't my mother. This came to mind again as I stood in front of the house in which my mother and I lived according to her own statements, if they were correct, and why would she have made false claims back then? The plan was that she could stay there with me for at least a short while, on this street, in this house. That, however, as good as didn't happen, so my assumption was and is, that the woman who ran the home—the home that apparently never existed in which I nevertheless was—that this woman *rocked* me. That's what's inside me and my guess is that this familiar yet unfamiliar woman was the sister of the farmer who kept burning my finger. *Where's your mother from, where*? This farmer had a map hanging on the wall, it covered the whole wall. I see it before me. *Heinz, where's Kirkenes, where*? He always had his cigar between his fingers. Takes my little finger. *There's Kirkenes.* I picture it before me. I stand in front of him, on the chair or on the table, depending. He bends down and takes hold of me and lifts me up. Then he hugs me, hugs me tight for a while. Then he holds me out, he holds me away from him, his arms outstretched, and we fly, *where will we fly to*, he laughs and spins and spins in a circle, we fly through the room endlessly, along the walls and over the countries and up to Kirkenes and down and up again. And the whole time—*where's your mother from, where*—he flies with me in his circles, lifting and lowering me, and with each circle I think, now he's going to toss me aside, now he's going to throw me against the wall. I didn't understand what was going on, but I knew what was coming, then he'd take my finger, mid-flight, flying towards Kirkenes, he'd take my finger and fly with it over the country and then in Kirkenes it burned. *Your mother's from there, from there.*

I thought of this then, in front of the house on Defreggerstraße, which had signified for my mother and me the end of the journey from Kirkenes to Hohenems.

We continued our walk. A few houses farther on, the archivist drew my attention to a woman looking over at us from a window on the upper floor. Her arms propped on a cushion, she surveyed the surrounding area. I turned away before our eyes could meet. Does the name Mina mean anything to you? the archivist asked.

We couldn't have been for very long here either, I said.

Maybe you should also see the hospital, he suggested, we'll go there through the *Jewish quarter*. And—*at the time, back then*—much of what went on *in the Reich* was also here, maybe even intensified, when you consider that there were only five thousand people living here. We had a Jewish community. There were only a few individual Jews still here, very few. But given the proximity to the border, many others tried to cross. The mayor stopped everything. It was strictly forbidden to shelter these people or help them in any way.

And *Pogromnacht*?

Not much happened in Hohenems. By then the old Nazis had moved into the Jews' houses. They'd manage to implant themselves there years earlier, after the owners had left the country. The synagogue was supposed to have been set on fire and blown up. The owner of the *Gasthof Habsburg* said that bales of straw had been placed around the synagogue to be set alight. But in the end, they didn't do it. They didn't want to risk having their own homes burn down with it. The mayor sent an inquiry to Munich, asking if it would be possible to spare the synagogue on *Kristallnacht* out of *concern for the party members* now residing in the Jewish houses. The request was granted. So much for the way these people treated their kind, the archivist said. As for the way they treated others, I think of Frieda Nagelberg, a Jewish woman the mayor especially had it in for. He personally sent the *yellow star* to the poor house where she lived and worked. He harassed her in every way possible for years, he even offered to pay for her ticket when she was deported. *I place the greatest importance on this last Jew leaving the Vorarlberg province and should her removal to Vienna be impeded by her travel costs, I am prepared to assume them*. He wrote this and achieved his objective. Frieda Nagelberg was *forcibly resettled*. As were the others. As were the Elkans, the last ones, they also ended up at an assembly point in Vienna and from there were sent on to Theresienstadt. Not one of them survived. In any case, this mayor was the man who was to have helped your mother on her arrival, if things went according to the plans of *Lebensborn* in Norway. This *request* was directed to him as leader of the local *NSV office*.

The alley we took opened onto a square. The houses here were also former Jewish homes taken by the Nazis, the archivist said and he pointed to a building on one corner of the square. That building with green shutters, he said, a national socialist *nuclear family* lived there, the hospital director, Doctor Neudörfer's superior, lived here. Doctor Neudörfer, the name doesn't mean anything to me, I asked, but he didn't reply. He pointed to a different building. And there, two doors down, is the building that housed the *Espionage Headquarters*, he said. From here, they crossed into Switzerland, probably to get instructions in the town of *Goldach* in order to investigate Jews who wanted to cross the border and so to expose possible escape plans. Because the Swiss still owned property on the Austrian side, they could cross the border and go back and forth unchecked. And this was used not just for escapes but also for espionage.

After a while we passed the *Gasthof Habsburg*. Those who wanted to continue on across the border stayed here, he said. This inn was the starting point for crossing the *Alter Rhein*. *Habsburg, Landhaus, Alter Rhein*, that was the way. Or farther on to Lustenau, where they tried to cross at the *Rohr*.

And now here—the end of the journey—or the beginning, depending on how you look at it, the hospital, the archivist said. At the time it looked the same as it does now. The *new* hospital was added later, on the back. Where the Russian barrack stood, there was a hospital for the forced labourers, for the Ukrainians, there were hundreds of them here. We'll go there now.

In Emsreute—that's a small village up there in the forest—Oskar Trebitsch, the renowned lawyer, the constitutional lawyer, was hidden for a time before he found the way across the *Alter Rhein*. Trebitsch was a Social Democrat, a Jew, he lived in Vienna and had to flee because the *Gestapo* were on his doorstep. He was told to contact someone in Lustenau if he wanted to cross the border. But it didn't work out, the person who was meant to guide him no longer dared. So Trebitsch came to Hohenems and tried again from here, the archivist said. In Hohenems, we had a doctor, Doctor Neudörfer, a *half Jew*, who was nonetheless protected by the Nazis because he treated them all. He worked as head physician in the hospital here. He was even occasionally called in for home-births. Oskar Trebitsch turned to this doctor after failing to cross the border in Lustenau. Neudörfer told him he could spend the night in a bathtub. That's what he did, he spent the night in a bathtub on the second floor, and the next morning, when he was leaving the building, he met a priest at the rear entrance, a chaplain. Doctor Neudörfer had arranged it. The chaplain took him up to Emsreute, where he'd worked as a priest, and hid him there in the sexton's house. He tried several times to find a way for Trebitsch to cross the border. But he couldn't find a way, so Trebitsch finally crossed the Rhein on his own and went on to Australia.

And Doctor Neudörfer? I asked.

Nothing happened to him, the archivist. The story with Trebitsch wasn't known at the time. Neudörfer did everything possible not be classified as Jewish. His *father* was Jewish. And had to constantly be on guard not to rub anyone the wrong way. He donated money to the NSV *Winterhilfswerk* funding drive and in this way, he *assimilated* himself—as I'd have done, the archivist said. And he was urgently needed in Hohenems because he was an outstanding doctor. In the *First World War*, he volunteered to fight against Russia. And during the Nazi years, he had a powerful supporter, Doctor Kopf, who was deputy state governor of Vorarlberg and took Neudörfer under his wing. There's a letter from State Governor Plankensteiner, who was also a district leader in the Nazi Party, addressing the question of whether Neudörfer could vote on the *Anschluss* in 1938—as a *half Jew*? In this letter, Plankenstier wrote that yes, he *could* vote because his *father* is Jewish, and his *mother* isn't. And, Plankensteiner wrote, even if I am normally inflexible on the *Jewish question*, I have to say that Neudörfer must be protected, the archivist told me. In 1933, he'd been named an *honorary citizen*. Normally, all honorary citizenships were rescinded but not his. He had this special protection. He was a timid man, cautious and always on guard, the archivist said, and so he was able to survive. But not because he was *cautious*, rather he survived because he was *necessary*. And he helped *a few others* survive.

Where we're standing now used to be the *main entrance*, he said. Where we want to go is the *rear entrance*. Let's go there now.

In a kind of lobby, from plaques on the walls he read several names of the hospital's founders and supporters, many of them Jewish residents of Hohenems. A few Germans were also benefactors, everyone joined forces to help, he said. After the *First World War*, there was a military hospital here. Now it's a palliative care ward. At the head of the corridor, he knocked in passing on a door. Behind this door was a bathroom, he said, and then a hospice room. And Oskar Trebitsch spent the night upstairs, on the second floor.

Past the hospice room, we came to a large hall. Here's the outpatient clinic, he said, patient admissions. In the hall that opened before us, countless people sat or stood, waiting to be called and sent to the various wards. The *outpatient clinic*—that's the *new building*, the archivist said, we just passed the *exit*, the former *rear entrance*. The spot where Chaplain Jakob Fußenegger waited for Oskar Trebitsch. From there, they went up to Emsreute. And on that day, a doctor who probably witnessed their meeting, is said to have threatened him, *be careful,*

Fußenegger, watch your step. That's how the chaplain described it later. He was being watched. A courageous man. He was arrested by the Gestapo and conscripted into the army.

But why in a bathtub? I asked.

He couldn't have stayed in a bed, the archivist said. There probably weren't any available and a bathtub would have been *less dangerous*. Keep in mind, the head of the hospital was a staunch National Socialist, an illegal, who also lived in the Jewish Quarter at the time, in one of the buildings I showed you. He was the official *director* of the hospital. Everyone was being watched. You had to report constantly. Every event, the smallest incident had to be reported. So it would have been *impossible* to let a Jew spend the night in a bed—within minutes the hospital administrator would have been informed, the archivist said and led me to a forecourt behind the building. This, then, is the *back*, he said. The building *there* in the centre of this square was the cloister of the *Catholic sisters* of Hall. The building next to it was the *old age home* or the *poor house*, where the Jewish woman Frieda Nagelberg had lived and worked. And *right next door* were the barracks. The *Russian hospital*. The women, the forced labourers from the East who were pregnant, had to bring their children into the world here. Or have them aborted. I know of a Polish woman, she'd gotten pregnant by a local. She was forced to have an abortion and so she was brought here to have the procedure done. And then she met Doctor Neudörfer, who advised her *strongly* against it and so she refused to have the pregnancy ended. That child is still alive today, the archivist said.

We stood a while in silence facing this square, in front of the barracks that no longer existed but had been there at the time.

Why are we here, actually, I asked.

Because I assume that Doctor Neudörfer was present at *your* birth.

So it's here that I was born. The same place my father died. A few years before that, my half-sister Ingrid got in touch, for the first time, to say that I had a father and three half-siblings in Hohenems and was invited to see them, *my father* would like to meet me.

They'd never sought contact with me and when I tried to establish contact, he refused. *Or measures would be taken*, I was told. They first got in touch after the theatre usher told them about me and that he knew me and that *I* claimed I was the son of a butcher named Halbsleben in Hohenems. And that led to this meeting. His name is right there on my birth certificate and his name is on this paper, on the travel itinerary. If this usher hadn't been in my theatre and hadn't happened to have been from Hohenems as well, then nothing would have happened.

I wrote the letter *after* I'd met him in the butcher shop. *I'd like to meet him*. Then the lawyer's letter came. Nothing after that—until Ingrid's call there was silence. I sent her the photograph—*mother with child*—and the *Lebensborn document*. She had no idea what *Lebensborn* was. He hadn't told her anything about that either.

You should come. Father would like to meet you. I drove there in my car. Got out. The street was empty except for one parked car, not where we'd agreed to meet, but close by. I waited for a while and nothing happened, and because nothing happened, I got out to have a look around and to stretch my legs after the long drive. Then I noticed that there were two people in the car, a woman and a man, an old man. They were deep in conversation and took no notice of me, so I passed the car and the row of houses until I came to the last house at the end of street. When I returned to the car and neither of them got out or made any kind of sign, I went up to the car and got in. He sat in the front seat. The woman sat behind the wheel.

Like my mother on our trip to Norway, now *I* sat in the back seat. I could see their eyes in the rear-view mirror. We sat like that for a long time. The car didn't move. When I opened the door to leave, the car started moving. At walking speed, they drove through the streets that I knew from when I'd come looking for him. But this time, we were traveling *together*, in search of *each other*, he wanted to *get to know* me, after all, that's why we were here. I didn't know where this journey would lead. Not to him, not to me, not to Norway and not to the farmer who kept burning me. This farmer could also have asked about my *father*, it occurred to me now. *Where's your father from, where?* To him it wouldn't have been as far as to Kirkenes; how many fewer of the *flying circles* he would have had to spin me in his arms.

How often I'd been on this trip to my *father* and how often *he* had visited me in dreams, when I lay awake in fear of him but also in longing for him to come and question me about my mother and listen to me tell him all about her. In my mind I was on the trip to Norway with my mother, past the matchstick trees that she liked so much. She left here as the *Norwegian whore*, she arrived as the *Nazi whore*. And with the one who was the cause of it all and the reason I was now sitting next to him: I was now traveling with *Private Anton Halbsleben*. I had my mother's *itinerary* with me and considered whether I should pull it out and show it to him and ask him about the next *stop* and where, in fact, this journey was leading, what he had planned for me and for us. *The Hohenems office is requested—should Miss Hörvold not meet her fiancé, Private Anton Halbsleben, in Berlin—to take charge of her until she is collected by her in-laws, the Anton Halbsleben family, Defreggerstraße 28, who have been informed of her arrival by telegram.*

I was thinking of the house on Defreggerstraße when our eyes met in the rear-view mirror. Our *gazes* didn't meet, however, because he was staring at the countryside and I was staring into the mirror, into his eyes.

What could he show me, what could he want to show me of himself, I wondered, and conversely, what would I tell him about my mother and perhaps reveal in doing so. I'd have shown him the house on Holzmühlestraße, the *Desser colony*, my stage in the courtyard, on which I'd created the first plays with *him* as an actor and with him—although I didn't realize it—as the all-powerful ruler that I portrayed and yet was trying to escape through these plays and with whose help I tried to kill my *stepfather*, with strength borrowed from my father, from my *real* father.

Would he show me *Emsreute*, or *Ebnit*, the place the Halbslebens came from according to the sawmill owner? Emsreute, where the Jewish lawyer Oskar Trebitsch hid from the Nazis, and Ebnit, where, years later, the mayor of Hohenems tried to hide from the French. One day they'd be buried next to each other in the Hohenems cemetery, he and the mayor. Where would he drive me during this *meeting*, which he decided on so suddenly after sixty years, I asked myself in his car, in which we sat in silence on an apparently aimlessly drive through the neighbourhood.

In front of the train station, we both looked over to the hospital, to the place where *I* was born and where *he* would die a few years later.

From then on, he kept staring straight ahead. Then, finally, he suddenly turned around and looked me directly in the eye and, a long time after we'd left Hohenems behind, he said into the silence, *you can call me Father*, but he said it without looking at me, as if he were saying it to his daughter sitting next to him, that's how it seemed to me. And as if *she* had read my thoughts, she said into the mirror, *Father would like to give you something*, and she shifted gears. *Father would like to give you something.*

In the meantime, we'd reached Dornbirn and the *Rote Haus*. I remembered that a *late reunion* between my mother and him was supposed to have taken place there, they'd agreed to meet there fifteen years after her arrival. I had a brief impression that we would stop there and get out, but Ingrid was just waiting for an old woman to cross the road. My mother had told me about the *Rote Haus*. That's where they'd agreed to meet. She was there, but he didn't come, that's the version I can still hear, the little she told me about him: I saw him again in Oslo and then, in the *Rote Haus*, I was going to see him again, but that didn't happen.

Dornbirn was the trip's destination and in Dornbirn our destination was a notary public, I now saw. In this notary's staircase, on the steps up to his office, I suddenly had the sense that we were back in the *Post*, my mother and I, in our first stop, and as if she would come flying down at me again any minute, as she did back then, to take me somewhere else.

In the notary's office, we sat across from each other. The notary talked, talked to me. What were my demands?

My demands *on what grounds*?

Then the notary pushed a note to me across the table with a number written on it.

Following this meeting, they drove me to the bank. I remained in the car. After a while he came out of the bank, carrying an envelope, which he put down on the seat next to me. *Keep an eye on the money*, he said.

We didn't see each other again, not before his death.

When the time came, the theatre was closed for the season, it must have been or I wouldn't have been in the area, on my *mother's turf*. It was evening, I'd called Ingrid and asked if she'd like to meet and she replied, if you want to see *Father* again, you'll have to hurry.

There was a grocer's shop nearby and I bought a few things that I thought he might like: juice, chocolate and biscuits. Then I stood at his bedside, I knew he could no longer speak, he had very large arms, he was all bloated. With one hand, he held onto the tubes, the fingers of his other hand patted the bed ceaselessly. I sat next to him and laid my hand next to his, near it in any case. Then I said, *Father, it's me*, I said. *Somehow*, his hand found mine and pressed it, whomever he was thinking of at the time. Five days later, he died, just as my mother had died five days after I visited her in the hospital. I left *her* sickbed too, for Münster, that time. I was playing in *Andorra*.

For a while, things were quiet around her, my half-siblings were grown, I was in Germany and her Norwegian friends were no longer around. And yet one day, the calm ended because she had become a mother again, a *foster mother* this time. And *her children*, Erhan, Orhan and Öner, the youngest; when I came home, whenever I visited, I could see how *she* experienced with them all that was impossible *for us* in the early years. And now, so many years later, the three still visit me the way they visited my mother until the end, and they tell me about that time and the present.

The *forced labourers*, the *foreign workers*, however they came here and for whatever reasons, when they stayed, they always remained *foreigners* and their children are foreigners' children and therefore also foreigners. Turkish *guest workers*, who fled the misery there in the hope of earning money and being able to return to their homeland before long—she took in the children of such *guest workers* and in doing so once again became the young woman who had to give up her child, for whatever reason, and she tried to make up or compensate for it by being there for these children.

Erhan, Orhan. And Öner. They still live in Lustenau, have their own embroidery factory, a small business, two machines, and they've since become fathers.

My mother was very close to them. When she was very ill, these children always stopped in to visit her and took her on outings, just as *we'd* always done with *them*. Her *madness* didn't matter to their parents. The main thing was that she took in the children. My mother took them in and they, in turn, became her only support. That may have been my mother's greatest friendship, her friendship with the Turkish family.

In the early 1970s, their parents had come from Turkey. They'd borrowed money for the trip from relatives. They'd gotten a visa in Istanbul and from there, they set out on their way. They travelled a full week, Erhan says, and in Yugoslavia, our mother said, let's stay here, it's beautiful here, too, she kept saying. Then, finally, they were in Lustenau. There was an old house that was empty; they lived in it for a long time, but it was like a stable, that house, they say. Some acquaintances from the same village in Turkey lived nearby. These neighbours helped them, they brought clothing, they brought everything the family might need. It wasn't just the people from Turkey, the Lustenauers were also helpful, especially the man they worked for, he helped them. Without him, they wouldn't have made it, they say.

Then my brother Erhan was born, Orhan, the middle brother, says. He was born on Pontenstraße, it was winter and the neighbours brought lots of clothing. And one day, a baby carriage was left outside the door. That's what their mother told them.

Their mother also worked in the embroidery factory. She had no time for a child. So the child was put *into foster care*. And because they couldn't find anyone for me, Erhan says, they sent me to my grandparents in Turkey. I was there an entire year, but we all couldn't bear it, so they brought me back. Then they found grandmother Oma for me. And once I moved in with her, I didn't want to leave, he says then. All three say this, that they don't want to go back to their own parents. She was always happy to see us when we opened the door, she always waited for us on the doorstep, Orhan says and he tells me only what I already know because it was no different with me and my friends.

She often told us about Norway, they say and I listen to them, hoping to learn more than what she told me about that time. She talked a lot about Norway, they say, but we were young and didn't understand everything. That they didn't have enough to eat is something she often said, they say, we were starving so we butchered hares, even I butchered hares, she always said. She told us a lot, but when you don't know the people being talked about—or Norway—we didn't know where it is. Now I do, but now it's too late, Öner says each time. If it were today, then I'd drive to Norway with her, he says. She liked to talk, she talked about everything. Even when we didn't understand much of what she said, they tell me. That is no doubt exactly why she was so ready to talk, I think, she could confide to their *child ears* without exposing herself or giving herself away, knowing that they wouldn't understand.

We were like a real family, they say. We didn't have any citizenship, not Austrian, but she never saw us as foreigners. For everyone there, she was the Norwegian woman, but for us she was our Oma.

And that's how it still is, they say. So we meet over all the years that are now gone. In their way, the three brothers have become *my brothers*, and at the same time have remained *my children*. They call me *Papa*, even though I know that they call every old man papa who is well disposed towards them and whom they like; still, every time it makes me happy.

Their parents came without a word of *German*. To earn money, to buy a tractor and a few sheep and cows—they wanted no more than that. Then the tractor was bought and they didn't go back. Their father bought property in Turkey. A house was built and sold. With the proceeds he bought property in another village and started building a house and when this house was built, he said, enough, now I'm going back with the children. And *only then* did our mother say, no, the children are too big, we're not leaving this country, she said. And so we all stayed. Our father rented an embroidery factory and made himself independent. So we also became embroiderers. Right after we finished school, after secondary school, we started working for him. At the time, you still had many opportunities as an embroiderer, there were lots of orders. Now the market is just Nigeria, Öner says, so I fly there, I'm in Nigeria once a month or every two months, he says. Twice a month I go to Dubai, to London. I make the sales. We create our own pattern, I offer it to them and if we get the order, we do the embroidery here.

Erhan was the first to go to my mother. Öner, the youngest, was in *foster care* in Feldkirch. My brother never wanted to be in his place of care, Orhan says, *I'm* the only one who was with Oma from the beginning, he says. On Friday, he was picked up. On Sunday he was brought back to her.

But then I also went to Oma with my brothers, Öner says. Until then, I always cried, they tell me. I don't remember any of it. My memory was blank. My first memory is of a meadow, he says, lots of flowers, large and small ones. Oma is sitting in this meadow and I'm sitting on her lap. She points at the flowers around us and tells me the names of the flowers. She tells me a story about each flower. The meadow blooms in her room, on the walls all around. We lived surrounded by these flowers and Oma told us stories about Norway and the flowers in Norway, she often talked about *frost flowers*. We went outside, in front of the house, and gathered flowers and grasses and asked her if they had these flowers in Norway too. In Norway they have all the flowers, she said.

We rode the bicycle, sat on the bike with her, all three of us at once. And we rode in circles around the house then out into the marshes and to the Rhine.

In the yard below, there was a tree and under the tree a bench, which she sat on and we showed her how well we could swim. The grass in the yard was never mowed because she loved the flowers. She would sit on the bench under the tree and watch us as we *swam* in the high grass, *crawled* actually. We swam to our parents' house on Pontenstraße, to the factory and farther on to Turkey, we went all the way to Norway like this, from her bench she would point in the direction she wanted us to swim. She taught us how to swim in the *Alter Rhein*, they tell me and they describe a tall, old tree surrounded by an anthill near which they would sit with her. A stick was tied to the tree, Öner says, which he would constantly beat against the dead tree. It made a sound, he says, that tree sounded like a drum. *Listen, the tree is talking*, she'd say then. And we wanted to know *what's the tree saying*—and she would tell us.

Whenever I came home, we'd take the boys on a trip. Often to a body of water, she came from water, so we'd regularly go to the lake, to Lake Constance. *To my fjord*, she said. We drove through the entire Bregenz forest, and the truth is that at the same time we were also driving into her past, which she revealed to us and didn't want us to notice. In retrospect, I often think that through these trips she might have been answering the questions I'd long stopped asking.

The epileptic seizures had stopped over the years. But then she had *internal* seizures. Her eyes would become fixed. She didn't look right or left, didn't blink, *nothing*. As if frozen. Then I knew that something was coming. When she'd then held the knife to my throat, I would just look into her eyes, and then, very slowly, she would lower the knife.

The boys thought it was a game. They knew she'd remain rigid for a while and then she'd pursue them. They used the time to disappear and watched from their hiding places as she tried to regain her composure.

These *seizures*—her eyes stop moving. In the middle of a glance. No movement at all, not even in her eyelids. Her body *moves*. Mechanically. Puppets move like that. Later, a trembling also set in. When I came home, now a memory—she's lying on the bed, her hand trembles, at first it was just a finger, then one hand, then the other hand, and so on. She was lying on the bed when I came. Then she stands up and becomes animated again. We set out on our way. The trembling has intensified, the *wobbling* as she called it set in—she *lay* on the bed, hands in her lap, one finger started twitching, it spread to her hand, up her arm, to the other side, and the last time I visited her, it affected her whole body and her head. But this *wobbling* was good for something. My brother had a child very late. And this boy who refused to go to sleep, her trembling arms would rock him to sleep. *It's the only way he goes to sleep*, she said.

When they came to get her, she could still walk down the stairs on her own, no one had to support her, according to *her Turkish children*, who accompanied her on her way.

I saw her in the hospital *two times*, Orhan says. The first time, *I* was the patient, I lay in a tent behind a thick pane of glass, and she visited me. She looked in at me through the glass. She pressed a hand against the glass and waved with the other. I wanted her to take me with her or for her to stay with me, to come in to see me. She wasn't allowed. But each time she left, she painted a flower on the glass. One day she finally did take me with her. On leaving, we wiped the flowers from the glass. We're taking them with us, she said, but they'll still be here *invisibly* for the next person who lie in your tent, only they will be able see them.

The second time, *I* visited *her*, he says, *I* came to see *her* in the hospital. She could no longer speak, but she waved. And she smiled, she's always smiling when I think of her.

Orhan called me, *it doesn't look good*. So I left Münster, while they were taking a vote in the theatre on whether I should be allowed to go see my ill mother, I left to see her. We were rehearsing *Andorra*. In the play, I was the innkeeper, so I closed up my inn and drove to see her. When I arrived, she was lying in a corridor, you couldn't lie in a corridor more miserably. I bent down to her and touched her very softly, on her shoulder.

Is it you, Heinz?

I drove back to Münster the same night. Five days later, the call came. A young couple was with me, neighbours in the building, they were about to leave on vacation and had brought me their cat, which I was supposed to watch while they were away and which I then adopted. I kept the cat, she stayed with me.

She died in the spring. That summer I went one last time to the building on Holzmühlestraße and the three rooms that she still had. There were masses of pills everywhere, they hadn't helped and yet she depended on them. A photograph of the two of us as *Mother Åse* and *Peer*.

This last encounter, the yard and the garden, the cellar, every day I was in one of the rooms, every day I went to her grave and talked to her and said goodbye to her or *tried* to say goodbye, because I didn't manage to, even today we still haven't said *goodbye* to each other and it's good the way it is, I still talk to her, even now I talk to her. Then I say, if I fail at something, I'd like to do it better, but I can't yet, I say. And back then, at her grave—I told her that I'd rather have gone *before* her.

I lay there, where I'd always pitched my bed, in her back room. When I woke, I could hear her breathing in the next room. Even today, thirty years later, when I can't sleep, when I can't *fall asleep*, she breathes me to sleep. *It's the only way I fall asleep.*

I took a few of her things back then, things that were insignificant but meaningful to me. A tin, an old coffee tin from the old days. In this tin, figures appeared in the coffee, in the *coffee substitute*: cowboys, Indians, bears and lions, hippos, lizards and hunters. *Playmates.*

One thing of hers that I still have is a satchel, a travel bag actually, it went with us wherever we travelled, on the trip to Norway and to *Valduna,* to Saarbrücken and on every outing with the children after that. Into that bag, I packed the things I took with me, sheets, towels, bedding. Her smell is still in these towels, after thirty years, she can still be found in them. Linens. Hand towels. And a headscarf that she wore in her last years. In these things, she's still with me.

And then there was also that fox fur, the *silver fox,* in which Halbsleben's relative, the sawmill owner, saw her as a 10-year-old in his grandfather's house and which I found among her clothing. He'd spoken of the *tall woman with the beautiful fur. I* never saw her in this fur. She had probably hidden it from Fritz, from my stepfather, and from all of us, nonetheless, it was a present from my father, a present from her *Norwegian time,* the only thing that still bound the two of them and therefore the three of us. I touched both of them at the same time when I stroked the dead creature's now mangy fur.

She would have had one reason to keep this fur over all the years. Our outings with the Turkish children came to mind, on which she would always tell them about Norway and in *very* rare moments about *him* too. When she did speak of him, she always soon broke off the story, but *without* any seizure that questions about him had *always* triggered before, but from the *silence* that set in you could tell that she'd been *fond* of him, and still was. She had *cared for* my father, I could feel it now.

I draped the silver fox around the shoulders of the cross on her grave. *Gerda Fritz, née Hörvold,* it said, now framed by this fur that had never warmed her when she was alive, or maybe it had.

Andorra had closed and yet it haunted me. I was the innkeeper in the play. A small role and yet big enough to kill a person and have someone else take the blame who will then die as a result.

It was the time when my mother lay in the hospital, in that corridor where I saw her the last time and from which I drove back to Münster, to *Andorra*, in order to kill with a rock the mother of the man I'd denounced. Because she was *Black*, because she was *from across the border*, a woman *who doesn't belong in Andorra*. And afterwards to escape responsibility with an excuse: *we were all wrong about this affair*, I say. They all say. No one wants to be blamed for what happened in front of everyone's eyes.

More than twenty years earlier the teacher had lived in a village in the hostile neighbouring nation, among the *Blacks*. With a woman *from over there*. They have a child, a son. The relationship falls apart, the man goes back to *Andorra*. He brings his son with him and tells everyone the boy is a *Jewish child* that he had saved from the anti-Semitic *Blacks*.

He marries an Andorra woman. Andri grows up as their *foster son*, believing that he's a *Jew* and so *different* from the others because anti-Semitism and xenophobia are pervasive in Andorra.

The invasion of the *Black troops* is imminent. *When the Blacks come*, they say, *then all the Jews will be rounded up right away*.

One day, a *woman from across the border* takes a room with me, in my inn. For years now she has known about the made-up story about the *saved Jewish child* and tries to reach her former lover, she wrote to him again and again but never received an answer. That's why she's here.

Why did you put this lie out into the world, she asks and immediately gives the answer. Afraid of her own people, she didn't dare stand by her child with an *Andorran*. Both of them had wanted to be *different* from their own people but couldn't do it. That's why she let him go back to *Andorra* with their son. And he wasn't brave enough either to stand by his relationship and child with a *Black woman*. *It was easier, at the time, to have a Jewish child*, he says.

At that time, I wasn't aware that *my* father had turned me into the son of a Russian in his stories and claimed that he'd brought my mother down from Norway *only out of pity* so that she wouldn't be murdered by her compatriots.

In the meantime, the *Black troops* have marched into *Andorra* and have begun ferreting out and going after Jews. Under the pressure of the events, the teacher admits the truth to his son. But his son doesn't believe him. No one believes him.

I thought of my mother at that point, every evening, in every performance I thought of the fact that until the very end, she was *always* in doubt about whether I was *her* Heinz, whom she'd brought into this world, or if maybe I'd been mixed up with another on a changing table somewhere. *I don't know, Heinz, are you the one or aren't you?* I thought of this. Back then. And now I think of Halbsleben, of the sentence he said to me years later. *You can call me father.*

No one can pick his own father, the teacher says to his son. *No one can choose his own father*, he says.

Whom would *I* have chosen as my father—I often wonder. *A few* of the people I met were fathers to me, each in his own way and without our realizing it at the time. The Capuchin friar out on the *Alter Rhein* was such a father to me. The teacher for whom I wrote my first life story was one. As was Herbert's father, Franz Jäger, who drove me to my *Transylvanian father*. Walter Fenz, the *submariner*, was a father to me. I sank with him in the factory, I was submerged in his *pompelusisch story, adiehala hadierscht*, and—with his intervention— I re-emerged as a quack in my first stage play. *Three Bags of Lies— Would Princess Roseblossom deign to take a deep breath?*

The chaplain who gave me his accordion was my father. As was the man in Wiesbaden with whom I lived and whose resurrected son I was for a time.

The cat I adopted from the young couple after my mother's death, it started with this cat. Since then, I've lived with animals. Currently, I have eleven chickens, one rooster and twelve cats. And mice too, hedgehogs. Animals come to me from all around.

The rooster, he's named *Ronnie* after my Norwegian cousin who took us in back then. He worked on an oil rig and he died on an oil rig.

This house is three hundred years old. It has been for sale since the first day I moved in. No buyer has been found yet, so we're still here, my animals and me. And should it come to that, my postman has an empty farmhouse just a few villages away, I can move in there and bring the mice, he says. But until then, we're staying here because it's good here the way it is.

The house isn't small but the apartment is just two rooms, a kitchen and the room I sleep in. The animals are always with me, every door has an opening, a hole they can go in and out of as they want.

The grounds are extensive and overgrown like it was on the *Alter Rhein* back then. The chickens only had a small enclosure in the darkest corner of the garden. Now they have lots of space. I put feed around the house, several times a day. The animals need me. And I can't live without these animals.

Ronnie doesn't like it when I talk on the phone. He thinks I'm talking to him and when he notices that I'm not, he won't put up with it. Just yesterday he jumped at my back. He also jumps at my face. When he does, he reminds me of the time with animals in Lustenau, back then, in Fritz's cellar.

The chickens like corn. Sweet corn. They like lettuce too, that is, sometimes they like it, sometimes not. The mice like to eat lettuce, the birds not at all. The pigeons here with me—no lettuce. And the crows that pass by—no lettuce. The crows love gouda cheese. And they get some. They also like bread, the crows do. The hedgehogs like cheese, they like bits of cheese. And curd cheese. Shelled sunflower seeds, the chickens eat those too. And the mice, the mice as well. I've got mice everywhere here, they have their very own cellar. The house has three cellars. In the film they shot here on the property, Father Otto Neururer was supposed to die in the middle cellar. The mice also like bread. And there are melons, the chickens like them. Seven, eight hedgehogs live on the property. They love melon and they also like bread.

For twenty years, the manure pile has been rising up to the sky. That's the chickens' favourite place. A crow also comes to see me, not just one, sometimes there are three of them. They like to eat curd cheese. Sunflower seeds too. The sparrows drink from the ash trays in the grass. And about ten pigeons live with me. They belong to a man in the neighbourhood who has become quite ill, so the pigeons are here with *me*.

I start the day by opening the hutch for the chickens, gradually they come out into the field, Ronnie draws attention to himself and I talk to the animals. I sit between the elder bushes in my arbour, they come and talk with me, one by one they pass by as if by chance and speak to me.

I open the hutch at quarter to seven. Six or six thirty would be better but I rarely manage that. Because first I have to clean the courtyard of feed that's no longer good from the previous day. When that's done, I open the door and they come out.

That's how it was in the film about Otto Neururer. Essentially it begins with me opening the door. The creatures were irritated because it was already after nine. But they came out into the field. In the enclosure I walk among them through the grass.

That's how it begins.

Who will I be in the film? I asked the director when he first told me about it. You'll play yourself, he said, you'll play your own story.

For years now, he comes and visits me in my arbour, then we sit amidst the chickens and talk. I've told him many stories about my Norwegian mother and the Austrian soldier, and I told him about *Lebensborn*. Often, very often.

As the Heinz I am in the film, I set out from my house, from here I set out looking for traces of this Father Neururer in places where he lived, but especially in his history that played out here, just a few stones' throws away.

The Nazis had their eyes on him very early on because he was a fervent opponent from the beginning. He had taken a stand for handicapped children, he had defended Jews. And the final reason, the grounds on which they took him was that he had dissuaded a young woman who was pregnant with the child of a divorced Nazi in the SA, whom she was meant to marry, from going through with the marriage.

Gestapo prison Innsbruck. Dachau. Buchenwald concentration camp. There a fellow prisoner had asked him to hear his confession. Neururer agreed even though a few other prisoners had advised him against it. Religious acts were forbidden in the camps under penalty of death. Neururer agreed to do it and ended up in the bunker as a result.

Inside here in my house, the middle cellar was going to be his prison cell after he'd been sentenced to death. That was the plan. But then, a different scene was filmed here. The director's son, who was twelve at the time, played the young Heinz. And my father, that is Fritz, was played by the director. He played *my* father. A bed was set up in the room, a small bed, on which this Heinz lay with his father sitting next to him, and all I know is that the point was that *the praying disturbed him*—I was told this in school. He sits on the bed next to me and tells me that I belong to the *Führer*, that I have to believe *in the Führer*, with my entire soul, and that I can only be redeemed *through the Führer*.

My stepfather, however, did *not* do that to me. For him, I didn't even exist. Except when he wanted my help butchering, then I was important to him, in the wash house in the cellar below, beyond that, he had nothing to do with me. And that made things difficult for me when they were filming because it meant that *I was playing myself*. My father was often mentioned in the film. But I didn't have one. I never had a father, never. A father *caressing* me, which Heinz's *father* does in this scene, that never happened in my life.

12.12.42

My dear Gerd has given birth to a boy. All are healthy, thank God.
I am the happiest man and as soon as I hear more, I will come myself or will write you a letter, my dear family. I wish you a happy and healthy Christmas and a good new year, dear Mother, Father and sisters-in-law and brothers-in-law.

Your happy Toni

News of my father's happiness reached me through a Norwegian cousin almost eighty years after he'd written down what come from his soul.

A few weeks earlier, this cousin had seen the film about Otto Neururer in a drive-in theatre in Oslo and set out in search of this person whose mother had been brought from Norway to Vorarlberg by *Lebensborn*. A relative from Kirkenes, one of my mother's many brothers' sons.

His search for my mother and me had begun much earlier. In his grandfather's estate, he'd found letters from my mother and my father and this film was a reason for him to contact me.

I knew nothing about him. Since the trip to Norway with my mother, there had no longer been any reason for contact with her family. Since to some of them, even thirty-four years after the war, she was still the *Nazi whore* and my cousin Ronnie had asked me to take her by the hand and start the trip home, I hadn't wanted to hear anything more from up there.

Sören. It was half a year ago that I first heard his voice. Now he calls. And almost every week, I receive a letter from '42 and the years after, letters written from Hohenems to Kirkenes, in which I *lose* myself again and again. Because I'm nowhere to be *found* in them. My mother isn't either, it's *another story* being told in these letters, a story that I didn't know.

Sören knows the *Norwegian* part of the *story*. He wants to learn the *Austrian* part. Between these two *stories* there's a border that's hard to cross.

For years, he has been tracking down the story of his grandfather, the mayor of *his hometown*, as he puts it, and the story of the mayor's daughter Gerd and her *Austrian* soldier. *Anton and Gerd*. He always speaks of *Anton and Gerd* when he talks about my father and my mother. He wants to understand how it all happened, he says. He wants to understand the conditions under *occupation* in his small Norwegian city. The population had completely fused with the German structure, he said. That's why his people lived closely with the German soldiers for four years. *Why* did the young women of Kirkenes get involved with the soldiers—you can't blame only the women, he says, because almost everyone was involved with the Germans. These men celebrated with them in their homes, were integrated into the families, all the while still being the enemy and remaining the enemy. The Norwegians *wanted* to fight them, but it wasn't for them to fight the war in their small city, he says. There are so many grandchildren *in my city* whose grandmothers bore children of German soldiers, he says. More than two hundred children of German and Austrian fathers were born in Kirkenes during the war. That's why he wants to understand what happened with Gerd and the *Austrian* soldier.

Anton Halbsleben. He has love letters from Anton, who wrote letters to the family in Norway, Sören says. He has letters from Anton's father, from his mother and from his sister, in which you can read how happy they were that Anton and Gerd found each other and that he would soon be a father. And he has letters from my mother, which she had also written after the war after everything had fallen apart.

He called for the first time in November. He was surprised to have actually found me, surprised that I wasn't just a character in the film he'd seen at the drive-in in Oslo. Since then, I receive these letters, he sends them in preparation for our first meeting and probably to see how I react. Recently he has also been telling me what my mother's

Norwegian letters say. There are so many letters, there must be hundreds of pages, he says. Most of them are in Norwegian. But the important letters from the war, that my father and his parents wrote, they're in German.

I know nothing about these letters, I said. What I do know is that she wanted to marry him, her *Austrian* soldier, but his mother objected to the marriage. And I also know that she was rejected by her Norwegian family, I told Sören.

It was very difficult for my grandfather, he replied. He was the mayor. Before the war, too. He was mayor of the city twice. And *after* the war, Gerd's brother was mayor. He was a Communist. There was also that orientation in my family, Sören says.

Uncle Fred. My mother's brother had fled to Russia. He worked for the Russian and for the Norwegian sides. He was responsible for making sure that information from Russia could get to Norway.

This gulf, this rift that ran through the family is what interests Sören. Gerd *went with the Germans*, she chose the Germans. Her brother *went with the Communists*. That was very hard for my grandfather to bear, he says. And *rejected*, yes, for a time that was true, when Gerd left Kirkenes and it stayed that way for the first years after the war. Only some years later, he'd wanted to *forgive* her and help her come home. But she was with Fritz by then and had two more children and either couldn't or wouldn't come back.

Maybe your grandmother wasn't the only one who objected to the marriage, maybe the SS did too, Sören suggests. When a Norwegian woman was pregnant with a German soldier's child, she was questioned to find out if her background was right, *ethnically* and *politically*. Gerd did not pass this *test*, he thinks. And Anton, perhaps he learnt in the course of the questioning that Gerd's brother was a Communist and that her father had been a Communist for many years, and perhaps after this he no longer *wanted* to marry her, Sören says, or maybe he wasn't even *allowed* to. Sören knows of several women from Kirkenes who had gotten pregnant by German soldiers and were not allowed to marry them. They were allowed to go to Germany, into the *Reich*, and have the child there, but they were not allowed to *marry*. Gerd may have been one of these women, he says.

I don't believe this. My father didn't need any help from the SS to *not* marry my mother.

In any case, he sent his birth certificate to my grandfather in Kirkenes so that he could arrange documents for their marriage. They did *try*. That's clear. But there was always some obstacle to the wedding, the date was set and then repeatedly postponed at the last minute, usually it was because of some documents that were apparently missing and had to be produced. They *did* try to marry. Both of them. The first letters from Anton's mother always mention—along with the imminent trip to Hohenems—the postponed wedding.

Hohenems 9.2.42

Dear Gerd and family!
Today we received a long-awaited letter from Toni, who has written us about your wedding, that it has been postponed on account of records. We are very sorry that there is such a long delay until you can come. We await you eagerly every day. I'm very worried about you, my dear. If only we had the great joy of seeing you soon. I pray every day for a happy and healthy encounter with you. And a safe trip for you, dear Gerd.

Anton's sister Klara also tries to reassure Gerd about the delay. *And you, dear Miss Gerd, seem to be having a bit of bad luck with the records needed to marry. But you know, this happens to everyone, as it did to me, too, but then suddenly the happy time comes when it all works out. I hope you can both come to us before you, dear Miss Gerd, give your dear Toni a strong boy or girl.*

My mother travelled from Norway to Hohenems to be reunited with my father, but in Hohenems they weren't reunited, in Hohenems they separated, I said to Sören.

She came to Hohenems, where she lived with Anton's parents. Says Sören. *It's in the letters*, he says. And Anton's parents, they were truly happy to have Gerd with them. That's what they say in the letters. How happy they are. He has read all the letters, he tells me, and every time he's surprised how positive Anton's parents are towards Gerd and the child and how eagerly *Gerd* welcomed into *Anton's family.*

I also found it strange to read my grandmother's letters after everything I'd heard about her and the role she'd played.

Hohenems 21 July 1942

Dear Gerd and parents and siblings!
I have taken the liberty of writing you a few lines to ask you how you are.

 Dear Gerd, since our dear son Toni has told us about your relationship, we'd like to ask you to come to us as soon as possible, as the long journey may later cause you discomfort and that would be terrible. Dear Gerd, if you have permission from your good and concerned parents, we ask you to come to us as soon as possible because there's no need to cause yourself further concern. The fact is, we do not see this as a misfortune. Most important—if our dear Lord sends Anton back home to us fully recovered, then everything will be right again. He will certainly provide for his wife and child. Dear Gerd, until Anton comes home and this sad war ends, we will take care of you as a good mother cares for her child. I will stand by you in good days and bad, because I understand what it is to be a mother. Therefore, dear Gerd, don't have any doubts or worries. Here with us, things will be as good for you as we can possibly make them. Dear Gerd, I feel how hard it is for your dear parents to let their daughter go out into the world without knowing us at all. But perhaps there will be a chance, after the war, for you to see your good parents and siblings again.

 Dear parents of Gerd, because our Toni has caused you such a great worry, we ask you to forgive our son the sorrow and tribulations that he has caused. We accept this lot in God's name, it will surely bring joy again.

A thousand heartfelt greetings, especially to Toni and Gerd, from his parents and grandparents and sisters.

Anton's sister Klara is also eager to meet her future sister-in-law. *Know, dear Gerd, that we are arranging things comfortably, so that we'll have a fine time together, so please don't worry at all, it would be pointless. And your dear parents and siblings should also not have any worries. If only I could tell you this in person. Now, to conclude, I'd like to request and ask if I might address you, dear Gerd, with that gentle little word 'Du'. We've become rather close, haven't we, Gerd? Forgive me for asking you so directly but it would make me so happy.*

These letters are from early on, when my mother was still in Norway. But then, something *must* have changed in the way they interacted in Hohenems. There's no mention of it in the letters, Sören says. Although, from the beginning, there are strange things in Gerd's letters, statements he doesn't understand, he says. When she writes, *I can hardly see my dear Heinz anymore because he's always with his grandparents.* She writes this very soon after the birth. Sören says that he doesn't understand.

I think she let her parents believe that she was still living with Anton's parents, even though for their family and for everyone else, she'd long disappeared.

For me, her letters are glimpses into her *lived* and her *described* reality. That these were two separate worlds was soon clear to me.

On the trip from Oslo to Hohenems, she was on her own, as she was later too, I said to Sören. I saw him again in Oslo, she always said.

But there are letters in which she writes *about her trip with Toni*. Sören says this. They both became seasick. It says so in her letters, he says. And *after* the trip, after *the great journey*, Anton spent several weeks in Hohenems on furlough, on *leave from the front*, before he had to return to his unit in Norway. And it's true. He wrote her parents from there. I've had this letter, too, since a few days ago.

16.11.42

Dear Hörvold family!

I send greetings in the name of my dear Gerd and my dear family at home. Despite all manner of difficulties, Gerd and I returned safely to my homeland. My parents were very happy. Yesterday I received a letter from Gerd in which she tells me that she's very happy there. She is a great joy to my parents, and she can make herself understood.

I don't think Gerd feels homesick; she writes that she has already settled in well. I'll tell you everything in person.

I've also settled in well over the eight days that I've been up here. It goes without saying that my deepest wish is for the war to come to an end. I now think of home more often. We all hope that God our Father will soon unfurl the flags of peace so the soldiers can go back to where the world stands open for us and where we may build a fortunate future.

Your Toni.

So much remains open. This letter, too, sheds a new light on everything. If what my mother says in the letters is true, then I'll have to live with this second half of the truth the way I've lived with the first half until now, knowing that a *whole* truth won't come from it.

Sören will visit me in a few weeks. Until then, we talk on the phone and I read the letters, another of which comes each week. He'll read her Norwegian letters to me, the way she read me *Peer Gynt* in those early years. Maybe I'll even understand them, the way I understood *Peer Gynt* back then.

Acknowledgements

This book would not exist if I hadn't met the actor Heinz Fitz, who gave me permission to freely develop this novel alongside his life story. For this I am grateful.

Particular thanks also go to the historian Arnulf Häfele, and all those who supported me with their knowledge, valuable information and suggestions: Heike Lindenberg, Trygg Hølvold, Önal, Hüseyn and Süleyman Kavlak, Alfons Peter, Otto and Veronika Hofer, Maria Wäger, Thomas Seifert, Klaus Rohrmoser, Josef Danler, Herbert Stocker and Julia Gschnitzer.

And Mercedes Blaas.

Alois Hotschnig